Memories:

EXPRESSION FROM THE WORD

A Tribute to Dad

ROSE LOVE

Memories: Expression From The Word
Copyright © 2022 by Rose Love

ISBN
978-1-958690-50-5 (Paperback)
978-1-958690-51-2 (eBook)
978-1-958690-49-9 (Hardcover)

CONTENTS

"But they that wait upon the Lord shall renew their strength: they shall mount up with wings as eagles: they shall run, and not be weary: and they shall walk and not faint," Isaiah 40:3

PREFACE

When I heard of Elder Baggett's death, to compile my notes into a book was like fire shut up in my bones. The Lord gave me the title and directed my thoughts as to how the book should be composed.

It is my prayer that *Memories: Expressions from the Word; A Tribute to Dad* will, first, save souls because the words will burn like fire in your heart causing you to seek salvation and second, revive the saints. May his teachings live forever and lead many generations to the Body of Christ.

He was the man of the hour. A man chosen by God to teach His people what thus says the Lord. He that has an ear let him hear what the spirit says unto the churches.

I have compiled bits and pieces of sermons/quotes and Bible class notes that I pray will inspire you.

ACKNOWLEDGMENTS

I want to thank each of my children for their inspiration and support. I give a special thanks to Mother Elaine Baggett and the Baggett family for allowing me to present this tribute. I want to give a very special thanks to those whose words are part of this tribute and those who at this point in time are reading this legacy.

I want to thank Sister Gaynel Williams, currently Young, who greeted me on my first visit to Morgan Park and made me feel loved.

To Elder Michael Hudson who prayed night and day in my home, thank you. "You are the thorn in my side," I would say to you: "Good," you always replied. Michael, your prayers helped me in my times of trouble. You were the ointment the Lord placed on the shelf for me to use. I enjoyed your testimony of how God saved you from drugs and the streets, and I loved seeing you shout and run around the church. "Great forgiveness brings great joy."

Also, I thank God for the late Elder Andrew Davis who was my mentor and Sunday school teacher and who always spoke uplifting words when I was down. Everyone wanted to be in his Sunday school class. He will be remembered as a man of God and I miss him dearly.

I want to thank David and Paulette Foster, who spent precious hours editing my material.

MEMORIES: TRIBUTES TO DAD

Suffragan Bishop Robert A. Taggett Sr
1919 – 2001

Memories and Love Are Gifts of God That Death Cannot Destroy.

TRIBUTE FROM A LOVING WIFE

First Lady Elaine Baggett, "Red": The promises of the Lord are of no avail to me except as I Apply, and appropriate them by faith. In my daily walk, I shall be victorious only to the degree that I trust in Him. He can help me only as I ask. He shall meet me at every point where I put action alone side my prayers. Only as I walk shall the waters of grief be parted before me.

As overburdened as the world is with trouble and sickness, God needs those who have proven His sufficiency in their everyday personal experiences to lead the suffering to the fountain of life. God needs those who have found Him as a burden bearer to help bring deliverance to the weary and the lost. I thank God that I am a vessel that He can yet use.

My husband, Suffragan Bishop Robert A. Baggett Sr., was a man who never complained but recognized in each encounter the opportunity to speak a word that may lead to someone's liberation. He knew that no case was too hard for God. He was rarely taken by surprise when God used him to change a pattern. My husband was a man of valor and great honor, yet a man of enormous humility; and he loved the Lord tremendously. He was a man who worked hard for Jesus and had a wonderful, exciting time rendering praises unto God. He worshipped God in spirit and in truth, and he allowed the Lord to use him mightily in the lives of many people because he gave himself unreservedly to God. I will always love my husband, Suffragan Bishop Robert A. Baggett Sr., and I thank God for a beautiful marriage of fifty-nine years.

Suffragan Bishop Robert A. Baggett And Sister Elaine Baggett

TRIBUTE FROM THE AUTHOR

My mother, who lived in Detroit, Michigan, died four years after I became a Christian. Upon her death, Mother Elaine Baggett (the former First Lady of the Morgan Park Assembly Church) took on the responsibility of being my mother, while Elder Robert A. Baggett Sr. became the father I never had. Their natural children, Eileen and Robert Jr., didn't mind as they embraced me as another member of the family, their new sister. Under their leadership of love, I grew and developed in the Lord.

As I reflect on my relationship with Elder Baggett, he always spoke to me as a loving father to his daughter. Sometimes he would say daughter, other times he would say, "How is my pretty Rose today?" His home was always available to me and he never denied me money in a crunch. He had a loving heart, which enabled him to be most giving. He was also unique due to the fact that he had a photographic mind. It was amazing to me how he would never forget a face.

One of my fondest memories is the way he stood on one hip, due to an arthritic condition that severely afflicted him in his later years. Yet, because he so graciously took his condition in stride, I admired him all the more. And the way he stood became a part of the loving man that he was. He was truly a man of God who always cared for God's people. Therefore, when he knew that his season of ministry was coming to an end, he sought God concerning his successor. Elder Baggett believed that God wanted the next Shepherd of our flock to be a man of God from Texas, in the person of Bishop William A. Ellis. As with any changing of the guard, some opposition arose. Nevertheless, as with any courageous leader, my dad stood in the power of our almighty God and Bishop William A. Ellis became our pastor. I believe that Bishop Ellis is our pastor because the LORD told Elder Baggett that Bishop Ellis was to be the next pastor of our congregation, and he refused to bow to the opinion and pressure that arose. Everyone that knew him will miss him and our love will always be with Mother Baggett and the family. Dad, my song to you is the "Battle Hymn of the Republic.

With love,

Rose Love

11-10-01
Dear Daughter Rose,
Praise the Lord. I'm very proud of you!
Just think, writing a book in memory of Dad!
God continue to bless you as "Author" (smile)
I will be praying for you too.
Mom

A HISTORICAL TRIBUTE
FROM A LOVING SON

As a child growing up in the Morgan Park Assembly Church, which later became—and is still—the Apostolic Pentecostal Church of Morgan Park, I was always drawn to the man I called "Uncle Bob." He became the assistant pastor after the current assistant pastor, Elder Val Johnson, now Suffragan Bishop Val Johnson, left to start work that is still flourishing in Peoria, Illinois.

Some of my earliest memories of the church were that Elder Baggett was an inspirational devotion leader and his wife, Sister Elaine Baggett, was the church organist. The music was always my first love, and perhaps that is why I gravitated to the Baggett so strongly. Their son, Robert Jr., was an accomplished musician and an athlete, so there was an attraction there also. To be able to assist Sister Rose Love in this endeavor is a joy that I cannot explain because of the man and woman who gave me my start in the Apostolic Pentecostal Church.

One Sunday, when I was a teenager, Sister Baggett chose me to direct the choir when our regular choir director, Aunt Dorothy (Dorothy Jackson, DD), was ill. I was overwhelmed, but at the same time, I felt that I had found what I loved and that was the music of the church. Elder Baggett was instrumental in encouraging me to go forward, and for many years I took lessons from Sister Baggett, but to no avail. I was simply not cut out to play the organ, but what was instilled in me was a love for the music of the church, and through the percussion instruments, I found my niche.

Upon his elevation to the pastorate of the Morgan Park Assembly Church in the mid-seventies, one of the first mandates given to me from Elder Baggett was to start a young adult choir. This choir grew to over one hundred young people and was known all over the Pentecostal Assemblies of the World as one of its finest choirs: and it was Elder Robert A. Baggett Sr. who had the vision and gave me and Sister Artis Fugate (now Wilson) the leeway to build this singing aggregation.

I take the time to recall Morgan Park's beginnings to enlighten those who are not familiar with the origin of the church's history.

In these messages, Sister Love and I have attempted to recapture the essence of his ministry, along with others who have labored so faithfully in this part of the vineyard.

Therefore, I purposed not to disturb his voice, his essence, or his gift of simplistically imparting the message of salvation. The teaching ministry of the Morgan Park Assembly Church/Apostolic Pentecostal Church of Morgan Park is tremendous, and it started back with our founder of Morgan Park,

District Elder Herbert Clyde Moore; But he was not alone; there were tremendous men and women of God who came through and added to this ministry, including Suffragan Bishop Val Johnson and his son, Bishop Byron Johnson, whom I count as a mentor and example of a true teacher and expositor of the Word; Elder Andrew Davis, who served faithfully as assistant pastor to Pastor Baggett; Elder Charles Dixon; Evangelist Ollie Lafayette, who was not only a prolific preacher, but also a songwriter and singer who recorded many songs and wrote many others; and many others whose names are not recorded here. To follow in this rich heritage of teachers and preachers is most certainly our current pastor, as he is one of the most dynamic preachers to ever pastor this church and is known throughout Christendom. Bishop William A. Ellis has continued with the vision of teaching by establishing an extension of Aenon Bible College at the Apostolic Pentecostal Church of Morgan Park to ensure that the strong teaching heritage of this church will maximize to its highest degree. As a son of the Park, I honor Bishop Ellis for his personal commitment to establishing the ministry as the 21st century millennium church. Nevertheless, as we journey, he has never failed to both remember the fathers and keep the "sound of Pentecost" alive.

I am truly humbled and honored to be chosen to assist in this project, and I hope that the "Memories" will richly bless your lives, as working on it has blessed me by affording me the opportunity to reminisce with great affection about my Uncle Bob.

Elder David E. Foster

TRIBUTE FROM A LOVING SON

Dear Pastor,

Please indulge me in my whim for a few moments. I have had it in my heart for some time to just drop you a few lines, not that I couldn't have said these things in person. I just felt that the leisure of writing would afford me a better opportunity to frame my words and thoughts.

I want you to know that I feel closer to you now than I ever have in the past. I appreciate your being someone I can call "my friend." I know that on occasion when you are busy and could have been doing other things, you took the time to talk to me, comfort and reassure me, just when it meant the most. I fully appreciate you for being a good teacher, not just in being able to communicate thoughts and truth by word of mouth but, most important, by being that living witness example. You are a very good role model. There are times during church service that I'm in a quandary as to what my reaction or position should be, but when I look at you, I gain some sense of direction.

I appreciate you most of all for being such a fine pastor, someone who cares for God's flocks of which I am the least. Your charisma and the characteristics mentioned above are the ingredients that make you the person and pastor you are. As I go on, I find there is much more, all of which makes me appreciate you all the more.

Elder Baggett, may God continue to bless you and make you a blessing unto all his people. Dad, I love you. I will never forget the encouragement and inspiration you have given me.

Always your faithful servant and son in Christ Jesus

Pastor Gregory Wells & Sister Joyce Wells

O'FALLON APOSTOLIC ASSEMBLY

403 South Lincoln Street
O'Fallon, Illinois 62269

Church Office: 618-632-9377 • Fax: 618-632-0497

Suffragan Bishop Gregory Wells, Sr.
Pastor and Founder

December 13, 2001

Rose Love-Woolfolk
From: Suffragan Bishop Gregory Wells, sr.

Dear Sister Rose:

Greetings in the wonderful Name of Jesus! What an unexpected pleasure to hear from you. It even a greater blessing as you have discovered this *"long lost artifact"*. I was amazed to see something that I had written so long ago and yet seemed to accurately convey my current sentiments in passing of our *"Dad"*, Bishop Robert A. Baggett.

I am so grateful that you thought enough to include this humble expression in your catalog of love for our late and beloved pastor. Please make the necessary corrections before printing as there are some typographical errors.

Words can't adequately express the fondness with which Dr. Baggett is remembered. I attribute much of my ministerial experiences and development as a Pastor is directly traceable to him and his example. Though he has gone on to be with the Lord, he will never be forgotten as long as there are *"Sons of Morgan Park"* who were spiritually conceived and nurtured in the loving environment that he hosted. May our Lord continue even now to bless his beloved family and all those his hands and heart touched. He was great man indeed a worthy laborer for the Lord. We shall miss him but we know that we shall see him again.

Please forgive the delay in returning this form. We are enclosing a picture and would appreciate it if you would mail it back at your earliest convenience.

Your Brother in Christ,

Suffragan Bishop Gregory Wells, sr.

Suffragan Bishop Robert A. Baggett Sr. with Family

Suffragan Bishop Robert A. Baggett Sr. with Friends

Suffragan Bishop Robert A. Baggett Sr. with Clergy

*How can we hear without a preacher? And
how can he preach unless he is sent?*

SECTION I

Inspirational Sermon Excerpts

***Unless noted, all messages are compiled from the
author's precious keepsake journals***

CHAPTER 1

<u>Focus Thought</u>

<u>*A Glorious Description of God*</u>

Nahum 1:2–3. GOD is jealous. The LORD revenges and is furious. The LORD will take vengeance on HIS adversaries, and HE reserves wrath for HIS enemies. The LORD is slow to anger and great in power and will not at all acquit the wicked.

Nineveh knows not the God that contends with her, and therefore is told what type of God He is. This glorious description of the Sovereign of the world, who was liken unto the pillar of cloud and fire, has a bright side towards Israel and a dark side towards the Egyptians. He is a God of flexible justice. He resents the affronts, open insults, and indignities done Him by those who deny His being or any of His perfections. He is angered by those who set up other gods in competition with Him and destroy His laws or ridicule His Word. God is jealous for his own honor in the matters of His worship and will not endure a rival; He is jealous for the comfort of His worshippers and He is jealous for His land.

He has fury, so the word says, not as man has it in whom it is an ungoverned passion, but He has it in such a way as becomes the righteous God. He has anger, but He is always Lord of his anger. We are not only told that God is a revenger, but that He will take vengeance. Whoever are his adversaries and enemies among men, He will make them feel His resentments; and though the sentence against His enemies is not executed speedily, yet He reserves wrath for them in the day of wrath.

This revelation of the wrath of God against His enemies is applied to Nineveh (verse 8). The Chaldeans' army shall overrun the country of the Assyrians and lay it to waste. "Darkness shall pursue His enemies," terror and trouble shall follow them whithersoever they

go. If they think to flee from the darkness, they will fall into that which is before them.

He is a God of irresistible power. If we look up into the regions of the air, we shall find proof of God's power. He has His way in the whirlwind and the storm (verse 3).

Wherever there is a whirlwind and a storm, God has the command and the control of it. He makes His way through it, goes His way in it, and serves His own purpose by it. If we cast our eyes upon the great deeps, we find that the sea is His. He made it and when He pleases, He rebukes it and makes it dry. He made proof of His power when He divided the Red Sea and the Jordan River.

Exodus 14:21–22. And Moses stretched out his hand over the sea; and the LORD caused the sea to go back by a strong east wind all that night, and made the sea dry land, and the waters were divided. And the children of Israel went into the midst of the sea upon the dry ground: and the waters were a wall unto them on their right hand, and on their left.

Joshua 3:13; 4:10, 11, 19 And it shall come to pass, as soon as the soles of the feet of the priests that bear the ark of the LORD, the Lord of all the earth, shall rest in the waters of Jordan, that the waters of Jordan shall be cut off from the waters that come down from above; and they shall stand upon an heap. 4:10 For the priests which bare the ark stood in the midst of Jordan, until everything was finished that the LORD commanded Joshua to speak unto the people, according to all that Moses commanded Joshua: and the people hasted and passed over. 4:11. And it came to pass, when all the people were clean passed over, that the ark of the LORD passed over, and the priests, in the presence of the people. 4:19 And the people came up out of Jordan on the tenth day of the first month, and encamped in Gilgal, in the east border of Jericho.

Let each one take his portion from this passage of scripture. Let the sinners read it and tremble; let the saints read it and triumph. The wrath of God is here revealed from heaven against His enemies; His favor and mercy are here assured to His faithful, loyal saints and reveals both His almighty power, making His wrath very terrible and His favor very desirable.

<u>What Do You Want Most in Life?</u>

Human nature never tolerates a vacuum. Denying your sexual passion will make you miserable, but sublimating it can bring you untold joy. Denying sinful pleasures is not the answer to growth in JESUS CHRIST. You grow by conforming to His character.

Romans 12:2. And be not conformed to this world: but be you transformed by the renewing of your mind that you; may prove what is that good, and acceptable, and perfect, will of GOD.

Galatians 4:19. My little children, of whom I travail in birth again until CHRIST be formed in you!

Grace gives you beauty and abundance in this life. That is why grace is Paul's first wish for everyone to whom he writes; money, health, happiness, or whatever else men deem good, constitutes only a part of grace.

God's favor has manifold parts. Why wish for a part of something when you can have all of it? Grace makes you conscious of an altered sense of values. It creates in you the sense of more pleasure in being purged than in being unclean, in being what God wants you to be, than in being what the world, the flesh, and the devil want you to be. After being conformed, you look back upon your previous life and realize how ugly it was. But it takes grace to put beauty in your life.

When you have God's favor, Paul said, you have everything, and it is free! You have open access to God, the Creator; He is your Father; you are His child.

What more could you want? Which is better, to be the child of the King with unlimited resources at your disposal or to possess only a certain number of stated privileges? Even Jesus, when He was tempted of the devil in the wilderness, could only be offered temporal things because the devil cannot offer anything eternal.

Romans 14:17. For the kingdom of GOD is not meat and drink; but righteousness, and peace, and joy in the Holy Ghost.

Do you know why Paul could say to the Corinthians, "Grace unto you?" Because Christ said it to him in the midst of his greatest trial:

2 Corinthians 12:9. And he said unto me, my grace is sufficient for thee: for my strength is made perfect in weakness. Most gladly therefore will I rather glory in my infirmities, that the power of CHRIST may rest upon me.

What Do the World and the CHRISTIAN Have in Common?

To answer this question, a definition of the word *world* as used in the scriptures is necessary. The following Bible quotations bring it into focus.

I John 2:15–17. Love not the world, neither the things that are in the world. If any man loves the world, the love of the Father is not in him. For all that is in the world, the lust of the flesh, and the lust of the eyes, and the pride of life, is not of the Father but is of the world.

James 4:4. You adulterers and adulteresses know you not that the friendship of the world is enmity with GOD? Whosoever therefore will be a friend of the world is enemy of GOD,

Evidently, the use of the word *world* in these scriptures refers to the ungodly system that holds the earth in its sway. When Satan tempted Christ in the wilderness, he paraded before him all the kingdoms of the world in a moment of time. In his clever attempt to thwart the plan of God, his insidious tricks associated two powerful forces with the world that are especially attractive to men: power and glory.

Luke 4:6. And the devil said unto him, all this power will I give thee, and the glory of them: for that is delivered unto me; and to whomsoever I will I give it.

Further, he intimated slyly that these forces were at his disposal and dispensable at his will. If Satan possesses such ability, certainly it is reasonable to suggest that every saint, regardless of how long he has been saved, needs to be on constant alert. Satan is sure to dangle these two alluring attractions before him in an attempt to frustrate his life and hinder his progress in the Lord.

The new saint should be reticent, silent, to partake of or participate in anything that threatens to involve him or make him a slave to this system of necessity. One must live in this world, yet we must be as pilgrims and strangers to it.

Hebrews 11:13. These all died in faith, not having received the promises, but having seen them afar off, and were persuaded of them, and embraced them, and confessed that they were strangers and pilgrims on the earth.

The apostle Paul instructed the Thessalonians to "Abstain from all appearance of evil" (1Thess. 5:22).

We're to shun everything that could be questionable as evil and disassociate ourselves from questionable practices that could lead to Satan taking advantage of it.

Paul depicts this truth clearly in instructing the church at Rome, "Let not sin." Putting it very bluntly, one must understand that you're at the controls and you hold your destiny in your own hands. We must come to grips with the world and recognize it for the system it is! John states, "And the world passes away, and the lusts thereof" (I John 2:17) Therefore, any association one has with it must be with this perspective in mind. The moment one becomes a member of "the church," he becomes indebted. He owes something to every living man! Paul declared that he was in debt to every man, regardless of his social status. Rich or poor, wise or unwise, civilized or barbarian, every man has a right to hear the gospel preached.

We pay that debt by several means. Some may be called to preach, others to be missionaries, still others will be used of God mightily in personal work. But all of us can labor in fasting, prayer, and sacrificial giving that others might embrace their calling.

It should be the earnest endeavor of every born-again Christian to diligently seek the Lord for Divine Direction, find the Will of God for your life, and pursue His will. Knowing that your contribution to the church; though small, is essential to its overall growth. You need the church to survive the onslaughts of Satan and build yourself up in God. Be in church every service, and when it is necessary that you miss, be sure you were not looking for a convenient excuse.

God&'s Provision for Man

God has not left us in this world of woe without hope. God has not left us in the quicksand of miry clay without a way of escape. God has not left us in this world of woe without a Savior. God has provided a substitute for man. A substitute is one who acts on behalf of another. In the book of Hebrews, chapter two and verse nine, Paul taught the truth of substitution when he said, "But we see Jesus, who was made a little lower than the angels for the suffering of death, crowned with glory and honor that He by the grace of God should taste death for every man."

Because of our sins, we deserved to die. God has sent the Lord Jesus Christ to be our substitute. God's Son tasted death on our behalf. Now we do not need to die eternally because payment was made for our sins. When the Lord Jesus Christ suffered on the cross of Calvary, He died on our behalf. At Calvary, Jesus died as our substitute.

The Lord Jesus Christ has taken our sins and removed the weight of sin from us. He became our sin bearer. Isaiah knew the Lord was to bear our sins and said, "But he was wounded for our transgressions, he was bruised for our iniquities: the chastisement of our peace was upon him; and with his stripes we are healed" (Isaiah 53:5).

Our Lord's back was lacerated, His brow was pierced with thorns, His hands were placed upon the cross and big spikes were driven in them. His feet were nailed to the cross. Why was He placed upon the cross in this manner? I believe the Word of God, which declares that He was placed there in this manner because He was our sin bearer and not because He had sinned, for "He did no sin neither was guile found in His mouth" (I Peter 2:22).

As human beings, we were sold to sin. We were slaves to sin and we were sinners by nature. We were sinners by practice and we were sinners by choice. We were sold into the depths of sin and under the dominion of Satan. We were in need of one who would ransom us and give us freedom. God, our heavenly Father, sent the Lord Jesus Christ to be our ransom.

We were in the world's pawnshop. We owed a debt we could not pay. Only one could ransom us and that one was the Lord Jesus Christ. He came from heaven's noonday to earth's midnight to pay the price of our ransom on the cross of Calvary, to ransom us from the penalty of sin and bring us into the possession of God.

How to Spend a Day with God

Psalms 25:5. Lead me in your truth, and teach me; for you are the God of my salvation; on you do I wait all the day.

Which of us can truly say the words of the text," On you do I wait all the day"? Which of us lives this life of communion with God, which is so much our business and blessedness? Yet, David's profession in the text shows us what should be our practice.

Our desire must be not only toward the good things that God gives, but also, and most important, toward God Himself. There must be a thirst for His favorite love, manifestation of His name to us, and the influence of His grace upon us.

Our delight in God must be such that we never wish for more than God. Believing Him to be the all-sufficient God, we must be entirely satisfied in Him; let Him be mine and I have enough

It is a child who waits on his father, in whom he has confidence and on whom he casts his care. Accordingly, as God's children, we, too, can expect all good to come to us from God. To wait on God is entirely and unreservedly to refer ourselves to His wise and Holy directions and disposals and to cheerfully accept them and comply with them.

We must wait on God every day; on the Lord's Day, on weekdays, on idle days and on dusky days; on days of prosperity and on days of adversity; on the days of youth and on the days of old age. We must cast our daily cares upon God and manage our daily business for Him. Through Him we receive our daily comforts, resist our daily temptations, do our daily duties in His strength, and bear our daily afflictions with submission to His will.

The eye of God is upon us. He sees all the motions of our hearts and sees with pleasure the motions of our hearts toward Him. This should lead us to always set Him before us.

"All things," even the thoughts and intent of the heart, "are naked and open unto the eyes of him with whom we have to do" (Hebrews 4:13). We must surely give account of ourselves to Him.

He continually waits to be gracious to us. He is always doing us good. He daily loads us with His benefits. His good providence waits on us all the day to preserve our going out and coming in. The Lord has angels who are appointed to be ministering spirits, to minister for the good of them who shall be heirs of salvation (Hebrews 1:14).

The more we discern the vanity and emptiness of the world, all our enjoyments in it and its utter insufficiency to make us happy, the closer we shall cleave to God and the more intimately we shall converse with Him.

We cannot, with confidence, wait upon God, but in and through a mediator. It is by His Son, Christ Jesus that God speaks to us and hears from us. ALl that passes between God and man must pass through that Daysman. The "Daysman" means mediator.

It is not the length or language of prayer that God looks at, but the sincerity of the heart is what shall be accepted.

If we continue waiting on God every day and all the day long, we shall grow more experienced and consequently more intimate in communing with God. "Therefore turn thou to thy God; keep mercy and judgment, and wait on thy God continually" (Hosea 12:6).

Creator Awareness

I Thessalonians 5:15. See that none render evil for evil unto any man; but ever follow that which is good, both among yourselves, and to all men.

Increased awareness makes a believer more sensitive to the Lord, the Word, himself, and the world. Though many believers know God, many seem to have a shallow and broken relationship with Him. Our senses are so bombarded by distractions of all sorts that it is hard to hear God's still small voice that speaks to our inner man.

1 Kings 19:11. And he said, Go forth, and stand upon the mount before the LORD. And, behold, the LORD passed by, and a great and strong wind rent the mountains, and brake in pieces the rocks before the LORD; but the LORD was not in the wind: and after the wind an earthquake; but the LORD was not in the earthquake: **19:12.** And after the earthquake a fire; but the LORD was not in the fire: and after the fire a still small voice.

We must be aware of what is being said by the world and our society. We cannot avoid contact with people for fear of being contaminated.

1 John 2:16 For all that is in the world, the lust of the flesh, and the lust of the eyes, and the pride of life, is not of the Father, but is of the world.

We can witness to our fellow man about our experience with God. Only if we listen to others with understanding can we expect them to listen to us. Men's (humanity's) problems and concerns are universal.

As we continue to read the Word of God and look at the world, our realization of God will grow. Nothing that happens comes as a surprise to God. Things are proceeding according to God's plan in precise agreement with what the scriptures describe as "the course of the age."

Matthew13:25. But while men slept, his enemy came and sowed tares among the wheat, and went his way. **13:29.** But he said, Nay; lest while you gather up the tares; you root up also the wheat with them. **13:30.** Let both grow together until the harvest: and in the time of harvest I will say to the reapers, Gather you together first the tares; and bind them in bundles to burn them: but gather the wheat into my barn.

And the victory of the LORD JESUS CHRIST will be fully shared by all who are His.

1 Cornithians 15:57 But, thanks be to GOD, which gives us the victory through our LORD JESUS CHRIST.

CHAPTER 2

<u>Focus Thought</u>

The Way of the Cross

<u>The Cross Divided</u>

There were three crosses upon the hill of Calvary. Two thieves were crucified with Jesus, one on the right hand, the other on the left. Jesus was in the center. One thief looked upon Him and railed on Him and said, "If thou be Christ, save thyself and us" (Luke 23:39). But the other answering, rebuked him saying, "Dost not thou fear God, seeing thou art in the same condemnation? And we indeed justly, for we receive the due reward of our deed; but this man hath done nothing amiss" (Luke 23:39–40). The second thief turned to Jesus and said, "Lord, remember me when you come into your Kingdom" (Luke 23:42). Jesus said unto him, "Verily, I say unto you, today you shall be with me in paradise" (Luke 23:43).

One was saved and the other was lost. The cross divides. The cross divides the crowd on Calvary's Hill. Not only two thieves were divided, but others also. The Lord Jesus, the Son of God, was the dividing line. Some were for Him, others were against Him. The cross divides all mankind today. Some are saved and multitudes are lost. The cross divides, for there is one Savior. Of one person it is said "thou shall call his name Jesus; for he shall save his people from their sins" (Matthew 1:21). The church cannot save, the ordinances cannot save, and sincerity cannot save. Jesus Christ is the only one who can save the soul. Therefore, the cross divides.

<u>The Cross Damns</u>

"He that believeth on him is not condemned; but he that believeth not is condemned already, because he has not believed in the name of the only begotten Son of God" (John 3:18). "He that believeth on the son has everlasting life; and he that believeth not the Son of God shall not see life, but the wrath of God abides on him" (John 3:18). Paul tells us that some people are enemies of the cross of Christ. Read Philippians 3:18-19.

The Bible declares that salvation is in Jesus Christ who died for us upon Calvary's Tree. The Bible declares that "He that believeth not is condemned already." The Bible declares in unmistakable terms, "Without the shedding of blood there is no remission of sin" (Hebrews 9:27).

The Cross Delivers

Now, let us turn to the word of God again and find words that will lift our hearts, make us to rejoice in that which we have in Christ Jesus our Lord. "For, I delivered unto you, first of all that which I also received; how that Christ died for our sins according to the scriptures" (I Corinthians 15:3). "And that he might reconcile, both unto God, in one body by the cross, having slain the enmity thereby" (Ephesians 2:16).

What does the word declare unto us? We are told that it is in the cross of Jesus Christ we have deliverance; we have salvation through the name of the Lord Jesus who died in our stead, we have salvation, freedom from hell, and deliverance from eternal torment and suffering.

In Christ, we have peace, freedom from worry, for we can rest and trust in the Lord and enjoy the peace of God. In Christ, we have a place, a home for eternity. Jesus said, "I go to prepare a place for you that where I am, there you may be also" (John 14: 2-3).

One! One! One!

The thinking of our generation is that it makes little difference what you believe or which church you attend. However, the scripture plainly declares that there is only one gospel that brings salvation to mankind.

Galatians 1:8. But, though we, or an angel from heaven, preach any other gospel unto you than that which we have preached unto you, Let him be accursed. (Our LORD, himself taught this fact…)

John 14:6. Jesus says unto him, I am the way, the truth and the life; no man cometh unto the Father but by me. The Apostle Paul strongly affirmed that there is but one church and one faith.

Ephesians 4:4-5. There is one body, and one spirit, even as you are called in one hope of your calling; one LORD, one faith, one baptism.

The preaching of the scriptures and the declaration of the holiness of God produces conviction in the heart of the sinner. Sinful and proud flesh cannot stand in the presence of a Holy God. This produces strong condemnation in one's life and drives him to his knees if he is really hungry for God. The first thing a sinner must do to find God is repent. Repentance is a turning around, resetting one's direction in life. In Acts, chapter two, the Apostle Peter's first response to those who inquired concerning salvation was "Repent." When a person has thoroughly repented, he is ready to be baptized in water in the name of Jesus Christ for the remission of sin.

Baptism is essential to salvation. Mark 16:16 states that "He that believeth and is baptized shall be saved, but he that believeth not shall be dammed." If baptism were not essential, Paul would never have commanded Cornelius and his household to be baptized in the name of the Lord Jesus (Acts 10:48). Through baptism, sins are washed away. Think about it! You have been baptized in Jesus' name and now your sins are forgiven.

When one has repented of his sins and has been baptized in the name of the Lord Jesus, he will receive the gift of the Holy Ghost (Acts 2:38). The Holy Ghost is the greatest gift that God ever gave to mankind. There is no experience in the world that is more exciting than receiving the baptism of the Holy Ghost. The Holy Ghost is not only wonderful, but it is essential to salvation (John 3:5, Romans 8:9).

This new life that we so greatly enjoy was made possible by Calvary. Calvary is the story of the death, burial, and resurrection of Jesus Christ. Calvary must be our experience. We must die, repent, be buried through water baptism, resurrected and filled with the Holy Ghost. Certainly, Calvary will ever be "dear" to the hearts of those who really appreciate their new life and salvation through Jesus Christ our Lord. For now we know that there is only one Lord, one faith, and one baptism! In the words of the song penned by André Crouch, "I shall forever lift mine eyes to Calvary, to view the Cross, where Jesus died for me. How marvelous His Grace that caught my falling soul. He looked beyond my faults and saw my need."

The Benefits of Justification

Romans 5:1. Therefore being justified by faith, we have peace with God through our Lord Jesus Christ.

The precious benefits and privileges that flow from justification are, such as should quicken us all to give diligence to make sure that we are justified. We must not fail to take the comfort it renders to us and to do the duty it calls from us. Let us never forget that the fruits of this tree of life are exceedingly precious.

Let me point out a few things we can learn from Romans 5:1.

We have peace with God.

The condition of man reveals his need of peace. It is sin that breeds the quarrel between God and us creating not only strangeness, but also an enmity. The holy, righteous God cannot in honor be at peace with a sinner while he continues under the guilt of sin.

Justification takes away the guilt and makes way for peace. And such are the benignity (graciousness) and good will of God to man that immediately, upon the removal of the obstacle, the peace is made.

For Abraham being justified by faith was called the friend of God (James 2:23) that was his honor, but not his peculiar honor. Christ called His disciples friends (John 15:13–15). Surely a man needs no more to make him happy than to have God as his friend.

Peace is brought to man through our Lord Jesus Christ! He is our great peacemaker, the mediator between God and man (I Timothy 2:5), that blessed Daysman, mediator, and His hands are upon us both. "He is Our Peace" (Ephesians 2:14). He's not only the maker, but also the maintenance of our peace (Colossians 1:20).

We have access to God.

This is the happy state of the saints! It is a state of grace, God loving kindness to us and our conformity to God. Now "unto this grace we have access," an introduction. This implies that we were not born in this state, but we are brought into it. "By whom we have access by faith," by Christ as the author and principal agent, by faith as the means of this access. Not by Christ in consideration of any merit of ours, but in consideration of our believing dependence upon Him.

Be of the Same Mind With One Another

Romans 15:5–6 Now the God of patience and consolation grant you to be like- minded one toward another according to Christ Jesus; that you may with one mind and one mouth glorify God, even the Father of our Lord Jesus Christ.

There is one outstanding lesson we can learn from history: Satan's primary strategy involves destroying unity among saints. He is the author of confusion, insensitivity, false doctrine, and church splits. Turning to the Bible, one soon discovers the power whereby Satan's strategy can be defeated. It's the power of being "one-minded" in the body of Christ.

Jesus prayed not only for the disciples, but all who believed in Him would be one (John 17:20–23). Jesus Christ's primary concern for His church stands out boldly in this prayer. It is a visible unity, a "oneness" that reveals the very essence of the gospel. And that essence comprises the fact "that God was reconciling the world unto Himself " (II Corinthians 5:19). Jesus Christ was indeed God in the flesh. If He had not been God, there could have been no plan for salvation. Christianity would be just another man- made religion.

I mentioned that Satan's strategy throughout church history has been to destroy unity in Christ's body. This makes a lot of sense from Satan's point of view. If he can destroy unity, he has destroyed the most powerful means of communication to lost humanity that Jesus Christ was God. When that message is obliterated or even blurred, we are doomed to eternal despair. Mankind cannot come to know God apart from coming to know Jesus Christ who was the Son of God (John 20:30–31).

We've noticed that Jesus' concern for unity in the church was also Paul's concern. Christ's prayer was also Paul's prayer. "Now the God of patience and consolation grant you to be like-minded one toward another according to Christ Jesus; that you may with one mind and mouth glorify God, even the Father of our Lord Jesus Christ" (Romans 15:5–6). Paul gave the same basic exhortations to the Ephesians and Philippians saints.

To the Ephesians, he wrote, "Endeavoring to keep the unity of the spirit in the bond of peace." And to the Philippians, he said, "Only let your conversation becomes the gospel of Christ; that whether I come and see you, or else be absent, I may hear of your affairs, that you stand fast in one spirit, with one mind striving together for the faith of the gospel" (Philippians 1:27).

I conclude that a functioning church must be a unified church. In fact, it's a reciprocal dynamic. Unity creates effective body function; effective body function creates more unity. Where there is unity, there will be a dynamic witness for Jesus Christ!

The Power of the Word of God

Elder Andrew Davis, Sermon Excerpt
Assistant Pastor
Morgan Park Assembly Church
January 12, 1975
Deuteronomy 8:1–3

The Bible is the written word of God, and all throughout there are just thousands and thousands of messages and sermons that can be brought forth from this Bible.

When God sends anyone, He sends him to talk to us from His written word. We know He talks; He talks to all of us and He talks in many ways. He talks orally, just as we can hear a man or woman talking in our ears, the Lord can do that. He also talks through His written word, through the Bible, if we would open our mind, and our heart: He can talk to us out of His Bible, out of His Word. Then, again, there is another way in which he talks and that is by His actions, His actions outside of us. He talks sometimes through the elements and He talks through the wind.

He talks through the waves, through the water and fire. He talks through the thunder, lightning and through the storms. He uses all of these things. He also talks through people outside of themselves. He talks through the things that we seek, even the ill things, the things that are not too good in our eyesight, the wars, the lying, God is talking, if we can but hear Him; and he is pleading with the people to draw closer to Him.

We know that we must be saved in the New Testament and must be kept by the word contained in the New Testament; but the New Testament is the Old Testament revealed.The Lord's Word went forth in the Old Testament first and sometime I just like to hear what He said.

"All the commandments which I command thee this day shall ye observe to do that ye may live, and multiply, and go in and possess the land which the LORD swears unto your fathers. And thou shall remember all the ways which the LORD thy God led thee these forty years in the wilderness, to humble thee, and to prove thee, to know what was in your heart, whether thou wouldst keep his commandments, or no. And he humbled thee, and suffered thee to hunger, and fed thee with manna, which thou knew not, neither did thy father know; that he might make thee know that man doth not live by bread only, but by every word that proceeds out of the mouth of the LORD doth man live" (Deuteronomy 8:1–3).

We know that God is powerful, omnipotent. He's everywhere at all time, omnipresent.

He knows everything, and that is omniscient. There's nothing that we can eat, drink, think, or go where God doesn't know about or hasn't made the way. But, sometimes we forget that God sees and we want to be reminded that God has a word and He uses His word for His purpose. He uses His word to help us if we would be helped. The reason for the forty years is because they couldn't hear His word.

He told them that he would bring them to the land that he promised their fathers Abraham, Isaac, and Jacob, but they rebelled in their hearts and wandered in the wilderness of Sinai forty years. He goes on to tell them that their raiment didn't even get old in the forty years, their shoes didn't wear out. He gave them food. He gave them water. They didn't do a thing but just wander, and they shouldn't have had to do that, but it was because of lack of faith on their part. He wants us first to know that He's God and beside Him there is no other.

He provided food for them every morning for forty years. It was called manna. After a while, they got tired of eating manna, they didn't want that light bread. They wanted some meat, and the Lord suffered them to have meat; and when it came down, it made them sick because it was not what God wanted for them.

The Lord said, be ye holy for I am holy. I don't like that part, but He says it anyway and He means it. Be ye perfect, as your father in heaven is perfect. Be righteous, be just, be peaceful, be of one mind and of one accord, let there be no division among you; these are the words of God. The Lord is requiring us to hear that we shall live. The thought in our text says man shall not live, does not live, by bread alone, but by every word that proceeds out of the mouth of the Lord does he live. Well, that was in the Old Testament.

God spoke into existence this whole world that we're living in. Everything that we see or touch, God spoke it into existence. He spoke when there was darkness here on the face of the deep and light came. He spoke and the earth came forth from the water. He spoke and the grass came forth. He spoke and the sun, stars, and moon came out. Through just speaking all things were manifested.

Then He spoke again and said, "let us make man" and this was a new thing. From the dust of the earth, He made man. And He made him in His image with a mind, with a spirit, with a soul different from the other animals He called forth from the water and earth. He created man special; and we are the most special creation that God has ever made or ever will make because He made him in His image and gave him authority and power over the earth that He had created. All he needed to do was dress these trees and to take the fruit of every tree in the garden with the exception of one.

God's word tells us and gives us one stipulation, don't touch or eat of the tree of knowledge of good and evil, which means that which Satan owns. There was an evil force in the world when man sinned and that evil force was bound up in this tree and man wasn't suppose to eat of it because when you eat that which that tree has, it becomes part of man.

We have that sin nature in us. We were born with it. But the word of God was — and still is, powerful and spoke to us, and it tells us today if we want to live, take heed to that which God has offered; the sacrifice that He gave for us to use that we might be free from our sin that we might live. We have a soul, and this is what belongs to God and this is what He's calling for.

The scripture says you're going to forever die or forever live; this is the result of the end of a life that we see here. We will be in heaven with the Lord or hell as we call it, the lake of fire, with the devil and his angels that the fire was made for. If we want to be saved from this fire or from this torment, we can be saved. God has no respect of person. You have to make the choice. The choice is from God's word. Faith is the element we must use in order to be saved.

When we see the life of Jesus, the Christ, we saw Him Holy and without blame in love walking right down here. God intended for Adam to be like that; but Jesus came down here and brought a state of righteousness into the world for people to live by and see how it could be done. Not only did He bring it, deliver it, but He provided a way for us that we can have it, and this is the good news.

What is the good news? The good news is the gospel of Jesus Christ. It's not the good news simply because He came down here; lived, did what was good, nor because he was crucified, buried, rose again, and went back to heaven. What makes it the good news stems from the fact that what he did, he did in my stead.

The gospel is that there can be deliverance from the state that we are in, from the point of view of the soul, the inner man. If the inner man is delivered, the outer man will automatically become better.

If I know the word of God, there's power in the word. When Jesus came, all He needed to do was speak. He spoke as the man of Jesus. He spoke and the dead were raised. He called Lazarus to come forth and He's still speaking today. He's speaking peace unto our soul by the Holy Ghost.

There's power to help us in our natural life; most of all, there's power to help us in our spiritual area. We have a conscience and God's going to trouble it sometimes if we don't obey because we know certain things to do; and when we don't do it, it becomes sin to us. I see young people more and more turning to the Lord because of what has happened in their life. In this nation, they have seen so much hypocrisy in high places and in every stage of life— in government, finance, labor, and politics. They tried the subculture of drugs, and they are still trying measures for so-called peace that isn't lasting. But there is one thing that will last forever and that is the word of God.

He sent his word to Peter one day. They believed that they were on one accord in one place and the Spirit of the Lord came down, the Holy Ghost, and filled them all. They began to speak with tongues, as they were filled with the power of the Lord, just because God's word said to do it. They recorded the result, and from that day until today people are yet receiving the Holy Ghost with power. It hasn't stopped.

He That Has an Ear, Let Him Hear What the Spirit Says unto the Churches

Elder Robert D. Young
Excerpts from 1976
International Evangelist
of the Pentecostal Assembly of the World

"He that hath an ear let him hear what the Spirit says unto the Churches; He that over comes shall not be hurt of the second death. And to the angel of the church in Pergamos write; These things says he which has the sharp sword with the two edges; I know thy works; and where thou dwells, even where Satan's seat is: and thou holds fast my name, and has not denied my faith, even those days where in Antipas was my faithful martyr, who was slain among you, where Satan dwells. But I have a few things against thee, because you have there them that hold the doctrine of Balaam, who taught Balac to cast a stumbling block before the children of Israel, to eat things sacrificed unto idols, and to commit fornication. So have you also them that hold the doctrine of the Nicolaitans, which I hate. Repent, or else I will come unto thee quickly, and will fight against them with the sword of my mouth. He that hath an ear, let him hear what the Spirit says unto the Churches; To him that over comes will I give to eat of the hidden manna, and will give him a white stone, and in the stone a new name written, which no man knows saving he that receives it" **(Revelation 2:11–17).**

Jesus Christ is the one that has passed through death but is alive forever more. Through His own might, He has caught the mind of John while being our captain. And He has decided to reintroduce Himself to John. John had known Him as He walked throughout the region of Palestine. He'd seen him break bread, fed 5 to 10 thousand. He has even watched Him give eyesight to the blind. He understood the awesome power of Jesus to speak and cause the wind and the waves to be still. He knew that Jesus certainly had the power to call them back from the dead. But now He is doing what his brethren, who used to be Saul, transformed into Paul, said he would to know Jesus and the power of His resurrection.

The message today is, God will bless us to hear what His holy men are saying. If not, we're going to find ourselves being hurt so dear by a hurt that will cover a form of every nation and every people that has not the power to accept the doctrine of Jesus Christ, that will cast them away from the second death that is certainly going to come.

There are a lot of people who have faith. There are a lot of people who have their faith; but Jesus is talking now from the standpoint of Himself, in His faith. There are those who have not denied my faith; and I say to you, whatever you have put your trust in, whomever you have put your trust in, hold on to the faith of Jesus Christ, everything else is going down.

Some folks are looking around for the Antichrist. I firmly believe that it will be a collective group of individuals that have become Anti- word, not really knowing that when you put aside the word of God, you have become Antichrist. It's the word of God and not the smile and not your lamp; it isn't the handshake, it isn't praise the Lord that will stand in that final day. It will only be to them that over cometh by the power of knowing the resurrected Savior and Lord Jesus Christ, and Him through the word of God. Some of us are going to have to become Anti- everything else but Jesus if we're going to make it.

There are those who would fool themselves, once saved always saved. I don't care what you do, but that's a lie. You cannot live like you want to live. You can't keep one foot in and one foot out. He said come all the way out, come out and be ye separated. He meant that. He says repent and I'll come and be with you. Repent, else I'm going to fight against you with the sword of my mouth. He that has an ear let him hear.

Every age isn't going to hear. Every messenger isn't going to preach the word of God. God said it's up to every individual, within every individual church age, to understand he's not getting any private interpretation or any private revelation. The message is given to every church age, Jesus Christ never changes. He says to him that has an ear let him hear what the spirit says unto the churches.

The Unmerited Favor of GOD

Elder Robert D. Young
Excerpts from 1976

Philippians 3:11–14. If by any means, I might attain unto the resurrection of the dead. Not as though I had already attained, either were already perfect: but I follow after, If that I may apprehend that for which also I am apprehended of Christ Jesus. Brethren, I count not myself to have apprehends: but this one thing I do, forgetting those things which are behind, and reaching forth unto those things which are before, I press toward the mark for the prize of the high calling of God in Christ Jesus.

Paul, after he'd reevaluated himself to a certain degree, said, I need a deeper knowledge of Christ Jesus. Paul looks at himself and says, now I've come to a point that if by any means I might attain unto the resurrection of the dead, I really want to be the kind of individual among dead individuals that individuals have no problem pointing me out and saying, he's alive in Christ Jesus.

Paul began to look back and recapitulate how it was when he was first placed under arrest. He says, "not as though I had already attained or were already perfect: but I follow after, if that I may apprehend that for which also I'm apprehend of Christ Jesus."

I can realize that I was apprehended; I was stopped on the Damascus Road. Suddenly, I was placed under the arresting power of the Holy Ghost. Now I know I have been stopped and I have been initially changed; but that's not all I want. I want to find out what was the initial origin of my calling in the first place.

Paul began to look back and look at his present life and forward to the future. If we're going to have a real revival, we're going have to do some looking back like Paul did and we're going to look toward the future like Paul looked. But we can't rest there alone because this is what Paul goes on to say; he says, "brethren, I count not myself to have apprehend but this one thing I do, forgetting those things which are behind and reaching for unto those things which are before."

Paul is saying, I looked back at those good old days of evangelizing, at those good old campaigns. I remember the time when I was in another prison. I was so happy, I had my feet, I had my hands; I remember singing alone with Silas. He and I locked up in this jail; we suddenly woke up with our back laid open. We had been beaten with many stripes. We started singing songs in our prison, and all of a sudden while we were singing an earthquake came. He can remember the good old days of being back there, but now he's in another prison.

Many of the children of God are forfeiting the blessing that God wants to give because they're living too much of their Christian life back in past victory and they're not having any present victory.

Paul says, I'm forgetting those things that are behind. And if you don't get to the point where you begin living in the present, you're never going to have any real good victory. It is good to be able to look back and see where God has brought you from; but looking back, you got to make up in your mind I'm going to look forward too.

Paul says, I remember what a terrible person I was. I remember how bad I was. I remember how I made the Christian people curse and deny Jesus Christ; but God saved me. He forgave me and I'm not looking back at that anymore. I'm forgetting those things, they are behind me; I am now a new creature in Christ Jesus.

Christ Jesus died on Calvary cross, and the blood of Jesus Christ washed away all my past deeds of wrong, every trespass, every sin is under the blood. If you don't look forward, you're not going to have any present victories because you keep on looking back in the past. Past victories, past failures, guilt complex, pride, all that is still detrimental. You can't live on how you used to be.

Paul said, I have some heavenly thoughts on my mind; I have a heavenly vision in my mind; I have a heavenly calling and that's what I'm pressing toward. I am pressing toward the mark, the mark for the prize. I really want to hear God say, when it's all over, you are a good and faithful servant. That is what we should be looking for, that is what we should be pressing for— the higher calling, the higher ground that is in Christ Jesus.

All some of us have on our mind is reaching from one paycheck to another or getting a car. Your vision is too low, too earthy. Paul says it all right, I got earthy vision while I'm down here; but I'm going to still look higher, I'm still looking, trying to see that fantastic light that caused me to be blind. I heard something, that's where I want to be.

<u>*But I Would Ye Should Understand*</u>

Elder Robert D. Young
Excerpts from 1977

Philippians 16:13–25. But I would you should understand, brethren, that the things which happened unto me have fallen out rather unto the furtherance of the gospel; so that my bonds in Christ are manifest in all the palace, and in all other places; And many of the brethren in the Lord, waxing confident by my bonds, are much more bold to speak the word without fear. Some indeed preach Christ even of envy and strife; and some also of good will: the one preach Christ of contention, not sincerely, supposing to add affliction to my bonds; but the other of love, knowing that I am set for the defense of the gospel. What then? Not with standing everyway whether in pretense, or in truth, Christ is preached; and I therein do rejoice, yea, and will rejoice.

Background Scripture: Acts 16:13–25.

Too many of the Christians or so-called Christians or so-called believers are trying to reach out for different facets of tranquilizers to get to see the tranquility, the joy of happiness that God intends for us to have no matter what has happen.

Christians are finding out more and more that God is giving permission for many of us to get in the area into the circumstances) that we've gotten ourselves into through disobedience and we can't get out (through our flesh we are trapped in bondage). Despite our desperation, I'm sure God isn't going to allow us to get out until He gets in our hearts what He wants to create. This is essential because God knows if He can't create in us what He wants to, then we will never be able to be delivered from the yokes that binds us. Yet, because of His endless love, God wants to set us free.

In Philippians 1, Paul states, "I would ye should understand, brethren, that the things which happened unto me, have happened and have fallen upon me so that the gospel of the Lord Jesus Christ might be spread further and further; so that even down in my bonds while I'm in my bonds in

Christ the glory of God is going to be manifested even in this place that I'm in."

I'm locked up, nobody wants to go to jail and in the beginning I could not understand why I was placed under arrest. Let me be free to soar like a bird. But after Paul began to recapitulate the high mind of God, that God's mind is higher than his mind and God's mind has decided that there isn't another man equipped with the desired inquisitive to really witness and minister behind bars like Paul.

So behind bars with a strange congregation, two Roman soldiers changing guard periodically, Paul has an opportunity to talk to two men who can't go anywhere. Every day is the same thing, the changing of the guards and Paul talking.

Now Paul says, I'm so happy that I'm now down here in prison that I don't know what to do. I've got these guys who can't go anywhere and the news of the gospel of Jesus Christ is going throughout the palace and he even heard that it got into the ears of Caesar himself.

CHAPTER 3

<u>Focus Thought</u>

Judgment

The man who is not a Christian might fear that which comes after death. Death is a word that is not commonly used in our everyday conversation. However, because the Bible speaks about it, we ought not to shun the usage of the word *death*. One may be very brave as we face the dangers of this world, but it's another matter entirely when we face the God whom we spurned in the land and His judgment. An individual would be a fool not to have any fears as he faces death without a SAVIOUR!

We have the Bible, the Word of God, which tells us exactly what comes after death. In that Book of Divine Authority, we are told that after death there, comes the judgment!

Hebrews 9:27. And as it is appointed unto men once to die, but after this judgment

Even today, judgment is going on everywhere. You cannot violate the laws of nature without suffering. There is no mercy in nature. Every civilized country has justice of some sort. They have courts and judges that try lawbreakers and punish them. Why? Because our very nature demands justice and judgment: there is something in man that cries out for justice and for judgment. It exists in the nature of God, and based on the fact that we are created in His image, He also placed the need for justice within us.

Aside from reason, the Bible teaches us that there will be a time of judgment. God is a God of love, but He is also a God of justice. When Adam and Eve sinned, He drove them out of the Garden of Eden. God branded Cain after Cain murdered Abel. He drowned the world in a flood; He burnt the cities of the plain; He overthrew many nations all because of sin. He still punishes sin. He says, "For I am the LORD, I change not" (Malachi 3:6).

Today is the day of grace and mercy. Today, you can cry out to God and be saved. God offers you tenderness and forgiveness now. At the Great White Throne, you'll find only fiery indignation and judgment. Time will have ended and every opportunity for salvation will be over. God's people, His saints, will be dwelling in everlasting joy and bliss while the devil's people, the lost sinners, will be standing before the Great White Throne awaiting judgment and damnation.

Your name may be written on a church role, but if you haven't been born again, you will stand with this group before the Great White Throne. Christ died on the cross for you. Now He asks you to give Him your life, that He might place it in His hands. There is salvation for you if you'll do this. If you don't come to Christ, there is nothing left for you but eternal death! Come to Him now and you'll never have to face the Great White Throne judgment!

The Cross of CHRIST

Book of Galatians

"But God forbid that I shall glory, save in the cross of our Lord Jesus Christ, by whom the world is crucified unto me, and I unto the world" (Galatians 6:14). No matter where one reads in the Bible, he comes to the cross of our Lord Jesus Christ. This is both true of the Old and New Testaments. The book of Galatians clearly illustrates that it is no exception. The cross looms large in its message and argument. In fact, one is impressed with the frequent reference to the cross. Paul knew the sufficiency of Christ's death and therefore makes it the dominating theme of the book. When Christ cries out from the cross, "it is finished," Paul comes along and declares what it is that is finished. He leaves no one in doubt as to what was provided by Christ's death and the shedding of His blood.

The Holy Spirit is ever seeking to drive home to the heart of men the value of Calvary by means of the written word! He wants all to see and understand that man's condition is so desperate that nothing short of Christ's work upon the cross can avail for him. The devil has so numbed the conscience of men that sin means very little. It is popular to speak of it as an error of judgment, a mistake, or a misstep that can be easily rectified. Not until we can say with David, "Against thee, and thee only, have I sinned," will we have the right perspective of sin. Sin is the transgression of God's law.

Preaching the cross in its entirety, as did Paul, does not make for popularity. If a preacher wants to count the favor of the multitudes, let him keep silent about the shed blood of the Lord Jesus Christ. Let him say nothing from the pulpit about the significance of the death of Jesus upon the cross! Christ dying for another is repulsive to the flesh and is the blow to human pride. The natural man is against this teaching. In spite of human revulsion, the cross is the divine magnet that draws men to God.

As we contemplate the cross in Galatians, I want you to note first that it is set forth as the place of substitution. Galatians 1:4, the place of identification; Galatians 2:20, the place of vision; Galatians 3:1, the place of a curse; Galatians 3:13, the place of redemption; Galatians 4:44,

8:23, the place of offense; Galatians 5:11; and last but not least, the place of glorying v. glorification. "But God forbid that I shall glory, save in the cross of our Lord Jesus Christ, by whom the world is crucified unto me, and I unto the world" (Galatians 6:14).

"God forbid", that anything should come between the cross and the Christians. Any other glory is sin! As it was with the Apostle Paul, who was captivated by the supreme merit of substitution, which God provided through Jesus Christ, so should it capture and hold us.

May God help us moment by moment to rivet our gaze upon the Christ of the cross! The cross delivers us from fears, from worries, from troubles; the cross gives us victory!

The True Heart

"Let us draw near with a true heart" (Hebrews 10:22). As we respond to that invitation, we become aware of some things that God seeks in us. Of these, the first is a true heart.

Just as we judge a man's physical character, his size, strength, age, and habits by his outward appearance, so the heart gives the real inward man, his character, and "the hidden man of the heart" is what God sees (I Peter 3:4). God has, in Christ, given access to His presence and His heart. No wonder that the first thing He asks, as He calls us unto Himself, is the heart, a true heart. Our innermost being must, in truth, be yielded to Him, true to Him.

True religion is a thing of the heart, an inward life. It is only as the desire of the heart is fixed upon God, the whole heart seeking to please God that a man can draw near to God.

The heart of man was expressly planned, created, and endowed with all its powers so that it might be capable of receiving and enjoying God and His love. Therefore, God asks for nothing more and nothing less than a true heart.

How many Christians still try to serve Him with religious ritual instead of with a true heart? I might say there are many! There are seasons for Bible reading and praying and church going.

"Let us draw near with a true heart." "Let no one hold back for fear—my heart is not true." The book of Hebrews, with its solemn warning and its blessed teaching, has come to bring restoration. When Christ said to the man with the withered hand, "stretch forth your hand" (Hebrews 12:13), the man felt the power of Jesus' voice and His eyes, and he stretched his hand forth. The hand was restored whole, like as the other. Do thou likewise, stretch forth, lift up, reach out that "withered heart" of your, and it will be made whole. In the very act of obeying the call to enter in, it will prove itself a true heart, a heart ready to obey and to trust its blessed Lord, a heart ready to give up all and find its life in the secret of His presence.

It is the heart God wants to dwell in. It is the state of the heart God wants to prove His power to bless. It is the love and the joy of God that makes us have a pure and true heart, so let us draw near to Him.

The Two Petitions of the Prodigal Son

"Father, give me" (Luke 15:11). "Father, make me" (Luke 15:19). The word *prodigal* means to be wasteful or spendthrift. I believe this lesson is not only meant to alert young people to think soberly, but adults as well. Take note of the two petitions this young man made to his father. The first was, "Father, give me the portion of goods that falls to me" (verse 11). The son was growing weary of the home. He acutely felt that he was missing things. The world was big, and the days were going by, and he was young. It is always better when the heart is young; the world always seems better and rich in visions and in voices.

The fatal mistake the prodigal son made was this: he thought that all he wanted was far off. He thought that the appeasing of his restlessness lay somewhere over the hills and far away. He was destined to learn better by and by. Meantime, he must have every penny for his journey, and he came to his father and said, "Father, give me." Note that there is no asking advice; there is no consulting of the father's wishes; there is no effort to learn the father's will in regard to the disposition of the patrimony. **It is the selfish cry of thoughtless youth** claiming what he feels is his birthright and demands to use it, as he will.

He got his portion and departed, and we all know the tragic consequences, not less tragic because the lamps are bright, the wine speaking, and the faces beautiful. The young lad tried to feed his soul through his senses, indulging in the lust of the flesh, the lust of the eyes and the pride of life. The Lord, in His own grim way, changes the cups, the music, and the laughter into the beastly routine of swine.

Then the young man came to himself. Memories of home began to awaken him. He lay in the shed thinking of his father. He began to feel sorry for himself, prayers unbidden rose within his heart, and now his petition was not "Father, give me." He got all he asked for and he was miserable.

His one impassioned cry was, "Father, make me. Father, make me a hired servant if you want to. I have no will but yours, now. I am an ignorant child and you are wise." Taught by life, disciplined by sorrow, scourged by the biting lash of his own folly, he instantly passed into submission. When previously, he knew no will but his own will, he must have it or he would hate his father. He reflected on when the only proof of love at home was the getting, of the things he demanded. But now his plea is "Father, make me anything thou pleases."

And surely it is very noteworthy that it was then he got the best. He never knew the riches in the home till he learned to leave his destiny to his father. When he offered his petition, "Father, give me," the story tells us that he got it and spent it. In a short time, he was in rage and beggary. It is not important that we go out into the world to appreciate the blessings of the Lord! This story is endeavoring to instill in each of us the importance of the second petition, "Father, make me." If we will but allow God to mold and make us, He will give us the best, a robe of righteousness, which is the garments of the honored guest and, a crown of life!

<u>Meekness and Quietness of Spirit</u>

I Peter 3:4. But let it be the hidden man of the heart in that which is not corruptible, even the ornament of a meek and quiet spirit which is in the sight of God of great price.

The fruit of the Holy Ghost teaches us to prudently govern our own anger and enables us to bear the anger of others patiently. Quietness is the evenness, the composure, and the rest of the soul that speaks of both the nature and the excellence of the grace of meekness. The greatest comfort and happiness of man is sometimes set forth by quietness. The power of a meek and quiet spirit gives victory. Meekness is a victory over ourselves and the rebellious desire we may have against God's Word.

What is meekness but the soul's agreement with itself? Next to the beauty of holiness, which is the soul's agreement with God, is the beauty of meekness. It is an ornament. The Bible speaks of it as an adorning much more excellent and valuable than gold and pearls. It is an adorning of the soul that recommends us to God. It is an adorning of God's making and accepting. It gives true courage.

True courage is such a presence of mind that enables a man to suffer rather than sin, to choose affliction rather than iniquity, to pass by an affront (although he may lose it and be hissed at for being a fool) rather than engage in a sinful quarrel. Calm are the thoughts, serene are the affections, rational are the prospects, and composed are the resolves of a meek and quiet soul. They are far from the pains and torture of an angry man. Meekness is the bond of Christian and saintly communion.

Love

December 8, 1976

The biggest, little word in the Bible is the word *love*. It is mentioned hundreds of times from Genesis through Revelation. We are told that, "God is love!" He is the embodiment of pure love. God is expressing His love for people all through the Bible.

Jesus not only died for us but rose from the grave because He loved us. The Bible speaks of our love for each other. We don't always see eye to eye or agree on everything, but there should never be a feeling of hostility, malice, or any other feeling that is out of context with the love of God.

Love is action. Each letter in love denotes spiritual steps in a Christian life.

L means long-suffering.

O is to overcome.

V stands for victory.

E is everlasting.

The fruit of the spirit (Galatians 5:22–23), "But the fruit of the Spirit is love, joy, peace, longsuffering, gentleness, goodness, faith, Meekness, temperance: against such there is no law".

True love has a way of causing one to think of oneself last.

Background scriptures:

Exodus 34:5-7 (v5) And the LORD descended in the cloud, and stood with him there, and proclaimed the name of the LORD. (v6) And the LORD passed by before him, and proclaimed, The LORD, The LORD God, merciful and gracious, long-suffering, and abundant in goodness and truth, (v7) Keeping mercy for thousands, forgiving iniquity and transgression and sin, and that will by no means clear the guilty; visiting the iniquity of the fathers upon the children, and upon the children's children, unto the third and to the fourth generation.

Isaiah 63:7–9. (v7) I will mention the loving kindnesses of the LORD, and the praises of the LORD, according to all that the LORD hath bestowed on us, and the great goodness toward the house of Israel, which he hath bestowed on them according to his mercies, and according to the multitude of his loving kindnesses. (v8) For he said, surely they are my people, children that will not lie: so he was their Savior. (v9) In their affliction, he was afflicted, and the angel of his presence saved them: in his love and in his pity he redeemed them; and he bares them, and carried them all the days of old.

Matthew 5:43–48. (v43) You have heard that it has been said you shall love thy neighbor, and hate your enemy. (v44) But I say unto you, Love your enemies, bless them that curse you, do good to them that hate you, and pray for them which despitefully use you, and persecute you; (v45) That you may be the children of your Father which is in heaven: for he makes his sun to rise on the evil and on the good, and sends rain on the just and on the unjust. (v46) For if you love them which love you, what reward have you? do not even the publicans the same? (v47) And if you salute your brethren only, what do you more than others? do not even the publicans so? (v48) Be you therefore perfect even; as your Father which is in heaven is perfect.

John 3:16. For God so loved the world, that he gave his only begotten Son, that whosoever believeth in him should not perish, but have everlasting life.

John 13:33–35. 33 Little children, yet a little while I am with you. You shall seek me: and as I said unto the Jews, Whither I go, you cannot come; so now I say to you. (v34) A new commandment I give unto you; that you love one another; as I have loved you, that you also love one another. (v35) By this shall all men know that you are my disciples, if you have love; one to another.

John 4:7–14. (v7) Beloved, let us love one another: for love is of God; and every one that loves is born of God, and knows God. (v8) He that loves not knows not God; for God is love. (v9) In this was manifested the love of God toward us, because that God sent his only begotten Son into the world, that we might live through him. (v10) Herein is love, not that we loved God, but that he loved us, and sent his Son to be the propitiation for our sins. (v11) Beloved, if God so loved us, we ought also to love one another.

12 No man has seen God at any time. If we love one another, God dwells in us, and his love is perfected in us. (v13) Hereby know we that we dwell in him, and he in us, because he has given us of his Spirit. (v14) And we have seen and do testify that the Father sent the Son to be the Savior of the world.

Romans 5:1–8. (v1) Therefore being justified by faith, we have peace with God through our Lord Jesus Christ: (v2) by whom also we have access by faith into this grace wherein we stand; and rejoice in hope of the glory of God. 3 And not only so, but we glory in tribulations also: knowing that tribulation works patience; (v4) and patience, experience; and experience, hope: (v5) And hope makes not ashamed; because the love of God is shed abroad in our hearts by the Holy Ghost which is given unto us. (v6) For when we were yet without strength, in due time Christ died for the ungodly. (v7) For scarcely for a righteous man will one die: yet peradventure for a good man some would even dare to die. (v8) But God commends his love toward us, in that, while we were yet sinners, Christ died for us.

The 13th Chapter of I Corinthians ends with the scripture, "Now abides faith, hope, charity, these three; but the greatest of these is charity," **love**.

The Lord Jesus gives us the ability through the Holy Ghost to love our neighbors, our enemies, and those that despitefully use us and to pray for them.

Loving those who mistreat you is not easy. We must not let the love of God that He shed abroad in our hearts go unnoticed. Let us praise and worship Him continually for His great love!

CHAPTER 4

<u>Focus Thought</u>

Lord, Help Me Build a Good House

"If you be for me: Lord, who can be against me?
1970's

Evangelist Ollie LaFayette
Missionary Encouragement and Exhortation
Missionary Dept. Chairperson
Morgan Park Assembly Church

The freeze may be on the monies, in terms of high interest rates and no mortgage availability, which may prevent many people from building a material house. But, in a sense, we're all still building. In fact, this is a good time to start and to continue to build; it is the accepted time.

When we hear God's voice, we should not harden our heart. The cry has gone out, saying, "Come, no money needed! Come buy without money, and without price" (Isaiah 55:1–2). The only hindrance is one's self; and we, personally, will be responsible for our own house. The material is available, no high interest rates to pay, no taxes, no house insurance, no protection against the many perils needed, and best of all, no mortgage payments. This mortgage holder has paid our full indebtedness for our homes. Thanks, be to God! The surest way to succeed is to let Jesus be Lord over your life. One needs knowledge and wisdom to build.

If Jesus is Lord of our house, He'll teach and give us the understanding and the wisdom to build a "good house." Proverbs 9:10 said, "The fear of the Lord is the beginning of wisdom."

To build, there must be some careful consideration given to whether you'll be able to finish your house. We can finish, and will finish the house, whether, it be good or bad.

Through wisdom is a house built and by understanding it is established (Proverbs 24:3–4). Matthew says, "whosoever hears the saying, instructions, of Jesus, and doeth them, is liken unto a wise man, who built his house on a rock but whosoever hears His sayings and doeth them not, was liken unto a foolish man who built his house on the sand" (Matthew 7:24–27).

There is no neutral ground. We are either building with the Lord of our house, or we're foolishly plucking it down by scattering instead of gathering with Jesus. The Lord of our house says, "Why call me Lord, Lord, and do not the things I say" (Luke 6:46)?

Keep Doing What You Can for Jesus

1980's

Evangelist Ollie Lafayette

We all, in a certain way, are missionaries because we've been commissioned by our Lord Jesus Christ to "go ye therefore, and teach all nations" (Matthew 28:19–20).

So our missionary work does not begin or end with a Sunday Missionary Service. It began when we were saved and were taught and understood God's word and will. As we read, fasted, and prayed, along with faithful attendance to Sunday school, Bible classes, prayer meetings, and worship services, we become missionaries.

By so doing, we learned and still hear the blessed Word of God, which is food for the soul, explained and expounded by Holy Ghost-filled preachers and teachers. We also learned by being doers and not hearers only. We also got involved in witnessing and testifying to others of this great salvation and what it means to us, along with being involved in doing good deeds wherever and whatever we can do to help in God's work.

A missionary is one who has received and allows the missionary spirit to operate in her heart. That spirit is the Holy Ghost, the Spirit of Jesus. Being in the pulpit on missionary day does not make us missionaries. We know already that God wants men to hear, and we know also that the harvest is ripe, but the laborers are few (Matthew 9:36–38). So we as fellow servants and co-laborers together in missionary work with God beseech and entreat others who've not put their hands to the work. Maybe we've started and sort of stopped along the way; or are just plain slothful. We must awake and stop sleeping and dragging our feet. Please don't bother or worry about titles or recognition. Just do the work. God sees us, and He'll reward every one according to their work.

Our foreign fields could be at home or wherever the need is. Just go where people are that need your help. Jesus said, "Follow me," and He'll make or teach us how" (Matthew 4:19).

<u>We Need One Another</u>

1980's

Evangelist Ollie Lafayette

The oneness and togetherness of us as workers together with God is one of the unique aspects of the church, Christ's body.

"So we,being many,are one body in Christ; and everyone members one of another" (Romans 12:5). Missionaries, we have a unique call. We are admonished to live a life, "walk worthy of the vocation wherein we are called," with all lowliness, humbleness, and meekness (Ephesians 4:1). The more excellent way is charity.

We, then, as workers together with God, encourage one another, not to receive the "grace" of God in vain or to no avail or profit, but to be diligent, striving to give no offense, stumbling, or hindrance in anything, so the ministry, our service for God's glory; be not blamed. There's no neutral place in the Lord; we're either with Him, or we're against Him.

Missionaries and workers, we have a high calling. Many are called, but few are chosen, not that God is slack, but on our part, man failed to obediently respond to God's invitation. But thanks be to God for the privilege of being a part of His body; therefore, "we'll forget those things which are behind and press toward the mark for the prize eternal life, of the high calling of God in Christ Jesus" (Philippians 3:12–19). We do not consider ourselves as having already attained, but we're pressing our way and reaching forth toward that end.

Enduring Beauty

1990's

Evangelist Ollie Lafayette

Christians are admonished to be an example for the world to follow. We are to show forth beauty and avoid all vanity, especially the superficial kind of beauty that does nothing for the inner man. Man cannot survive nor walk with God when he holds hand with vain persons (Proverbs 12:11, 28:19).

God created man subject to vanity, but God also subjected man to hope (Romans 8:20). It is our privilege to choose the temporal or the eternal. The description of the missionaries' beauty for today is in Colossians 3:12–17. Here Paul tells us to "put on" bowels of mercies and other great qualities of God.

We are to put on kindness, humbleness of mind, meekness, and long-suffering. This kind of beauty needs no moderation. We can put on as much as we need. Plenty is needed, and plenty is available. God is plenteous in mercy (Psalms 86:15, 103:8). His mercy endures from generation to generation and forever.

CHAPTER 5

<u>Focus Thought</u>

<u>The Thankful Spirit</u>

"And let the peace of God rule in your heart, to which you are called in one body: and be thankful" **Colossians 3:15**

The people to whom this was addressed were mostly people in very humble circumstances; many of them would have been slaves. Their lot best was not a pleasant lot. Their privileges were as few as their enjoyments. Always in a heathen city, to be a Christian aggravated everything. Yet, the singular thing is that when the apostle wrote to them, in such letters as this to the Colossians, he never seems to have offered them his sympathy. When death enters any of our homes, the mourners receive many kind letters.

The truest sympathy sometimes is not pity. The truest sympathy sometimes is encouragement. The hand that helps is the hand that points the way to new fidelity and service. And so the apostle never hesitates, even when writing to the Colossians' slaves, to urge them to embrace the grace of thankfulness.

In doing so, he, of course, was calling them to what he himself practiced so magnificently. You have but to think of him in the prison of Philippi singing praises there to God at midnight to see how he practiced what he preached when he urged the Colossians to be thankful (Acts 16).

And so I would like to dwell a little upon that most important Christian duty. I begin by saying that true thankfulness is probably harder and rarer than we think. All of us abhor ingratitude. We speak of it in the severest terms. I have heard Christian people say that they could forgive anything except ingratitude. And yet, as life goes on, we often find that the sin that is easiest to commit is that of not giving thanks.

On one occasion our Savior healed ten lepers. He healed them all and healed them equally. Yet of the ten, only one came back and showed himself a grateful man. In times of special mercy, of course, thankfulness is an instinctive feeling. There are hours when it is natural to weep and hours when it is natural to cry, "Thank God." When a child is rescued from a burning house, when a man is rescued from a watery grave, when the cries are past and the light of life comes back as in a fever or from the surgeon's knife, then in a rush of feeling from the depths, pure fervent gratitude is born. And God, who may have been long ignored, is recognized again in that glad moment as He who was wounded and yet it is His hands that make us whole.

To be thankful in the sense of scripture is to be thankful every ordinary day. It is to bear our routine burdens cheerfully, to meet our common sorrows without murmuring. It is to feel the hand of God in everything, to acknowledge the ordering of His love and know that for us there isn't anything common or unclean. He who is rarely clean is not a clean man, and he who is rarely thankful is not a thankful man.

Thankfulness, when you come to think of it, really depends upon our view of God. As is our God, so is our gratitude. If all that happens to us comes by chance, of course, no man can be grateful. Gratitude is not a duty then, for there is no one to be grateful for. Nor can gratitude ever be a duty if God were only a cold and distant spirit who would take no personal interest in man. Two duties lie within power of man: fortitude to face the worst and resignation in the worst. Because of that, the old pagan world's noblest gospel known to them was that of fortitude and resignation. Then came the gospel of the Lord Jesus and resignation was swallowed up in thankfulness, not because their lot was different, but because their God was different.

Jesus had the spirit of thankfulness. On these occasions in the life of Christ, we find Him giving thanks to God. Once He gave thanks for common things, when He broke loaves of bread upon the mountainside. Again, He gave thanks for ordinary people, in that God had revealed His secret unto babes.

And again in the darkest hour of His life, that night He was betrayed, He broke into such glorious thanksgiving as one who heard it could never forget. When the cross was waiting for Him and all its agony, the spitting, the mocking, the grave, when all He had toiled for seemed to be in vain, we find our Savior thankful and pouring out His gratitude in prayer. As

Jesus walked, let us so walk and be thankful as He was. Not for the glad things only, but for the shadowed things. Not for the great things only, but for the common things. Why? Just because God is love and in love all things work together for our good!

47

The Greatest Facts of History

I Corinthians

15:12 Now. if Christ be preached that he rose from the dead, how say some among you that there is no resurrection of the dead?

15:13.But if there be no resurrection of the dead; then is Christ not risen:

15:14.And if Christ be not risen, then [is] our preaching vain, and your faith [is] also vain.

15:15. Yea and we are found false witnesses of God; because we have testified of God that he raised; up Christ: whom he raised; not up, if so be that the dead rise not.

15:16.For if the dead rise not; then, is not Christ raised:

15:17.And if Christ be not raised, your faith is vain; ye are yet in your sins. 15:18. Then they also which are fallen asleep in Christ are perished.

15:19. If in this life only we have hope in Christ, we are of all men most miserable.

5:20. But, now, is Christ risen from the dead, and become the first fruits of them that slept.

15:21.For since by man came death, by man came also the resurrection of the dead.

15:22.For as in Adam all die even so in Christ shall all be made alive.

15:23. But every man in his own order: Christ the first fruits; afterward they that are Christ's at his coming.

15:24. Then comes the end; when he shall have delivered up the kingdom to God, even the Father; when he shall have put down all rule and all authority and power.

15:25.For he must reign till, he has put all enemies under his feet.

15:26.The last enemy that shall be destroyed is death.

Two great facts about Christianity make it different from all other religions of the world. First, Christianity is virtually bound up in a person, the Lord Jesus Christ, God's only begotten Son. He was born of a virgin, died a vicarious death on a shameful cross, was buried in a borrowed tomb, rose from the dead, and ascended into heaven from whence He will return someday to set up His everlasting Kingdom.

Yes, Christianity centers on the person of the Lord Jesus Christ. One can be a good Buddhist and know little or nothing of Buddha or a good Mohammedan and know little or nothing of Mohammed. These religions are forms of rituals, but one has to know Christ before becoming Christ-like or a Christian. You can't be a Christian without trusting, loving, and following the Lord Jesus. Christianity is Christ! It is a joy to know that being born of the water, baptism in the name of the Lord Jesus and the Spirit, gift of the Holy Ghost, makes us a special people, saints, who receive the Lord Jesus Christ as a person, not by accepting a creed or a system or form of ethics. "But as many as receive Him, to them gave He power to become the sons of God, even to them that believe on His name" (John 1:12). Jesus says, "Behold, I stand at the door and knock; if any man hear my voice, and will open the door, I will come in to him, and will sup with him and he with me" (Revelation 3:20).

The second fact of being followers of Christ that is different from every other world religion is that its founder is alive! Although Christianity was founded over nineteen hundred years ago, its founder still lives. Jesus lives today! The other religions, Islam and Buddhism, cannot make this boast because the graves of the founders tell the fact. But where is Jesus buried in Jerusalem? You hear the angel from heaven saying, "He is not here for He is risen" (Matthew 28:6).

The cross is the symbol of the Christian religion, but it is an employ cross, not a crucifix. He is alive; our leader, our founder is alive for ever more. He is the very center of our religion, a living Lord, a Savior who saves and keeps, walks and talks with His people. The resurrection of the Lord means more to the Church than anything that has happened, ever. The Bible teaches that it is the most significant event in the world's history. Paul stated that "if Christ is not risen, we preachers are false witnesses." If Christ did not rise from the dead, all would be lost and all preaching and witnessing in vain. Our faith is of no value and we are still in sin if Christ is dead.

If any person would read and examine the Bible with an open mind, the Holy Ghost will lead him into the truth of the resurrection and the effect it had on his followers. I'm so glad that Jesus rose from the dead! In doing so, He made our salvation possible. I'm glad that I can follow Him in this world and look to go up, Rapture, someday to be with Him forever. So I say as I think of the resurrection and all it means, "Hallelujah, Hallelujah, what a Savior! There is no greater fact in History for this is History."

Christmas:
The Advent of the Christ

The Gospel of Matthew begins with a genealogy, then the story of the birth and infancy of Jesus. Jesus was born in Bethlehem. This was the most wonderful event of human history, the coming of the Son of God in human flesh into this world. Love was born that night. True, there was love in the world before.

Mothers loved their children, friend loved friend. Natural affection was common, but the love that we know as Christian and saintly love had its beginning with the birth of the Lord Jesus Christ. It is well for us to note, however, that the historical event of Christ's birth is not that which saves us. He must be born again in us.

This greatest event in history made little stir in the world. Usually when heirs to a throne are born, whole realms ring with joy, but when the Messiah was born, there was no earthly rejoicing. A few humble shepherds came and looked with wonder on the newborn babe, who lay in the manger with the mother, Mary, and the father, Joseph, beside Him. The Jews had been looking for their Messiah but did not recognize Him when He came. His advent was quiet. There was no blare of trumpets. Noise and show are not necessarily accompaniments of power. The most useful Christians and saints are not those who make the most noise and show off their works, but those who in humility and simplicity, unconscious of any splendor in their faces, go daily about their work for their Lord and Master.

The scene when the wise men found the Child King was very beautiful! They saw only a little child lying in a young mother's arms. There was no crown on His head.

No glory gleamed from His face. His surrounding was most unkindly, without pomp or brilliance. The Child did nothing before them to show His royalty, spoke no word. Shall we be behind the wise men in our admiration?

The wise men did more than adore, they opened their treasures and offered gifts of gold, frankincense, and myrrh, which they brought all the way from their own home. The sincerity of their worship was thus attested by the costliness of their gifts. The treasures they had brought were of great value, the most costly things they could find, the best they had to give. It is not enough to give Christ a homage that costs nothing. He asks for our gifts, the offering of our love, our service, the consecration of our lives. Giving is the test of loving; the measure of our loving is what we are willing to give and sacrifice.

There are many ways of laying our offering at the feet of Jesus Christ. He Himself does not need our money, but His cause needs it. The extension of His Kingdom in this world at home and abroad requires money and must be brought by His followers. Those who have no interest in the saving of others; in the sending of the gospel to those, who have it not, have not themselves really tasted of the love of Jesus Christ.

We must remember there is all the difference in the world between Christmas and Christ. God is offering you the greatest Christmas gift of all, His dear Son! "Thanks be unto God for His unspeakable gift" (II Corinthians 9:15).

Christmas and the Saints

"And she shall bring forth a son, and you shall call his name Jesus, for he shall save his people from their sins" **Matthew 1:21**

The cause for Jesus' birth was salvation. He was born to save. We must keep this always in mind. It is good that a time is set for us to remember his birth, but we know Him as the mighty God, not the babe in the manger. The announcement of the angel to the shepherds carried a message much beyond the birth. Luke 2:8, "I bring for you good tidings of great joy." The gospel, which is the death, burial, and resurrection, is good tidings and the good news of God's gift of salvation. The gospel brings great joy. Therefore, if we keep the cause in mind, we know how far to go.

It is traditional for people to give willingly and to show love at this time of year, but as children of the King, we should give whenever there is a need and to show love all year long. It is traditional to put up a tree with beautiful lights in and outside, but what about the light of Christ that is in you? Are you letting it shine? That is the real way of letting all know that you believe and know the Christ of Christmas! Our giving should be done in simplicity, not expecting anything in return. Saints should not overdo anything.

We don't have to go out for the most expensive gifts. The simple things mean so much when given in love. Some people give only to those they are sure will give to them. In our giving, let us remember those who are less fortunate; that kind of giving brings real joy. It is rewarding to see that gladness and to know it's because you cared.

<u>On Easter, Remember Jesus Christ</u>

Don't Be a Pilate

April 22, 1984

"When Pilate saw that he could prevail nothing, but that rather a tumult was made, he took water, and washed his hands before the multitude, saying, I am innocent of the blood of this just person: see you to it," so Matthew 27:11– 26 describes our Lord's appearance before Pontius Pilate, the Roman governor.

Jesus, who had the power to judge the world, allowed Himself to be judged and condemned though, "He had done no violence, neither was any deceit in His mouth" (Isaiah 53:9). He, from whose lips Pilate and Caiaphas would one day receive their eternal sentence, suffered silently an unjust sentence. These silent sufferings fulfilled the words of Isaiah 53:7: "As a sheep before her shearers is dumb, so he opened not his mouth." Because of His blood, we who have been born again owe Him all our peace and hope in a turbulent, un-restful world.

Pilate appears to have been inwardly satisfied that Jesus had done nothing worthy of death. We are told distinctly that he knew that for envy they had delivered (Jesus). Left to the exercise of his' own unbiased judgment, he would probably have dismissed the charges against our Lord and let Him go free. But Pilate was the governor of a jealous and turbulent people; his great desire was to procure favor from them and please them. He cared little how much he sinned against God and conscience, so long as he had the praise of men.

After a feeble attempt to divert the fury of the people from Jesus to Barabbas, and a feebler attempt to satisfy his own conscience by washing his hands publicly before the people, he at last condemned the one whom he himself called a "just person." He rejected the strange and mysterious warning that his wife sent to him after her dream: he stifled the remonstrance, objections, of his conscience. He delivered Jesus to be crucified.

Despite all that Pilate and others did, let us remember our Lord Jesus Christ and what this day, Easter, means to us. We can recall in His word, "no man takes my life; I have power to lay it down and power to take it up again." Praise the Lord! Let me give you a few more reasons we can and should remember Jesus Christ on Easter. The infallible truths of the word of God; the Bible, says, and we quote, "The veil of the temple was rent, Old Testament saints were resurrected, the centurion gave his testimony. Jesus was placed in a tomb, sealed with the guards placed there." Thanks, be to God, we can remember, He rose from the dead and from the grave. The women saw the place where He was. Peter and others encountered the Risen Lord! His resurrection is the basic message of the gospel.

On Easter, remember it is not in the new clothing and the beautiful colors that are worn, it is not in the abundance of food on the table, it is not in colored or dyed eggs, it is not in the bunny rabbit, but it is in Jesus Christ! Remember it was He who said, "I was dead but behold I am alive forever more." Because He lives, we the saints of God live also.

Let not this day be the only day we remember Jesus Christ. Let us not forget the cross of Calvary. Let us not forget His suffering and dying for us whom He loved and gave His life for our sin. I trust we will remember Jesus Christ who is the author and finisher of our faith not one day, but every day, as we walk with Him. On Easter, remember Jesus Christ!

CHAPTER 6

What Love

May 7, 1995

"I am crucified with Christ: nevertheless I live; yet not I, but Christ lives in me: and the life which I now live in the flesh I live by the faith of the Son of God, who loved me and gave himself for me." (Galatians 2:20)

Henry Drummond wrote a little book titled *The Greatest Thing in the World*. He stated in his writing that love is the greatest thing in the world. The 13th chapter of I Corinthians ends with the scripture, "Now abides faith, hope, charity (love), these three; but the greatest of these is charity" (love). If the question should arise in our minds as to where this thing called love came from, we would find that it is God Himself! God is love. Note: 1 John 4:8, 16, "All love, both human and divine, comes from God."

The Apostle Paul suffered for Christ as no other person did. Why did he do it? Because he loved Him! Paul said, "All that has happened to me doesn't matter. I gladly suffer all things for Christ." True love has a way of causing someone to think of him or herself last. Jesus is the greatest person who ever lived! His greatness is summed up in St. John 3:16: "God so loved the world, that he gave his only begotten Son, that whosoever believeth in him should not perish but have everlasting life."

As we look toward the cross, our minds should reflect on the many stripes laid on His back. In the book of Isaiah, we read, "By His stripes we are healed." When they laid the cross on the back of our Lord Jesus Christ, they did not realize what they were doing. They were so obsessed with crucifying Him that they were not aware that they were laying their sins and ours upon Him! Our Lord bore the sins of many, yet He never said a word.

Some may ask why. The answer is all because of love. "Greater love hath no man than this, that a man lay down his life for his friends" (St. John 15:13).

In Psalms 40, David says, "He brought me up also out of a horrible pit, out of the miry clay, and set my feet upon a rock, and established my goings. And put a new song in my mouth, even praise unto our God." We that are sanctified by the blood of Jesus and filled with His spirit have this testimony that we are new creatures in Christ Jesus because of love, His love!

Verse for the Week

"As the Father hath loved me, so have I loved you: continue you in my love" (John 15:9).

Thought for the Week

Christ is coming back to earth one day and we ought to love His appearing.

Called unto Holiness

March 20, 1983

"God hath not called us unto uncleanness, but unto holiness" **I Thessalonians 4:7**

A man's calling is that at which he works and by which he is distinguished from others who follow different callings. The saint's calling, the one thing that he is to work at and that will distinguish him, from those who are not saints; is holiness. He must say, even though we are not happy about saying it, many who have embraced the holiness of God are not holding up the standard that God has set for true holiness. Some did run well, but something hindered them. In their eyes things went wrong, they were disappointed over someone they had trusted, they were perplexed by controversies around God's truth. They lost hope and consequently forgot their calling, called unto holiness!

Because God has called us to holiness, we have this assurance of victory: "Faithful is he that calls you, who also will do it" (I Thessalonians 5:24). This verse of scripture tells us what God is, what God has done, and what God will do. It tells us that God is faithful. The faithfulness of God is the assurance that he is altogether prejudiced in our favor. A prejudiced person is one who prejudges a case before it is investigated. Our case was prejudged at Calvary, where the Lord Jesus Christ bore the iniquity of us all.

God has called us with an ever-present call. God's people are called of Jesus Christ; they are called according to His purpose. We cannot have fellowship with God if we harbor evil in our hearts. Because the Lord Jesus Christ has called us unto holiness, He expects His dear children to be in the world, but not of the world. The Lord Jesus Christ expects us to be a light to those who are in darkness.

God paid the price for us by shedding His precious blood on Calvary's cross, and after returning back to heaven, sent the Comforter, the Holy Ghost, that we would be the recipients of spiritual power to live a holy, sanctified life right here on planet earth.

God will do what is necessary to make this holy calling effectual. He does not merely call us and leave matters there. We are called unto holiness, a life of dedication, love, peace, joy in tribulation, fasting and praying, and more. We may ask; who is sufficient for all of this? The answer comes in the good news of I Thessalonians 5:23: "And the very God of peace sanctify you wholly; and I pray God your whole spirit and soul and body be preserved blameless unto the coming of our Lord Jesus Christ."

We who know Christ can be thankful and grateful that He thought enough of us and gave us the blessed privilege to be called unto holiness! Those who do not know Christ have the opportunity to come unto Him so that they may be called unto holiness!

Verse for the Week

"But now being made free from sin, and becoming servants to God, you have your fruit unto holiness and the end everlasting life" (Romans 6:22).

Thought for the Week

The holiness of God shows the vileness of sin. God's word and holiness are the only true sources of guidance from sin.

A Vessel Chosen and Fitted

October 21, 1984

"Then the word of the Lord came unto me, saying, before I formed you in the belly I knew you; and before you came forth out of the womb I sanctified you, and I ordained you a prophet unto the nations" **Jeremiah 1:4–5**

The account of Jeremiah's call to the prophetic office is very instructive and deeply interesting. The thoughtful reader feels at once how intensely human was the man and how condescendingly gracious the Lord. On the part of the servant there is the feeling of backwardness and trembling when commissioned to be the bearer of God's message to His backslidden people. It would be at best a thankless task; for people away from God, ignorant of their condition, do not, as a rule, show much gratitude to the man who seeks to turn the light on and manifest things as they really are.

It is, generally speaking, a far more pleasant and agreeable task to preach the gospel to poor lost sinners than to minister to the needs of wayward saints. None but a man who is himself very low before God can accomplish it successfully. If I would wash my brother's feet, I must stoop to do it. But in this, as in all true service, one's reliance must be upon God, who never sends a messenger without putting in his mouth the word he is to speak and never bids one to undertake a service for which He does not qualify the servant. Every minister, regardless of what part of the vineyard he is toiling in, must recognize that he is a vessel of mercy who has received a message from the giver, that he may give to the receiver the word of the Lord.

The Lord spoke abruptly to Jeremiah and said, "Before I formed you in the belly I knew you; and before you came out of the womb I sanctified you, and I ordained you a prophet unto the nation." Jeremiah is given to understand from the first that it is the eternal, omniscient, omnipotent Jehovah with whom he has to do. The natural man may shrink from this, but the saints should delight just in the thought of God, His word and His messengers.

The words, "Thou shall go to all that I send you, and whatsoever I command you, you shall speak. Be not afraid of their faces, for I am with you, says the Lord, you are to be an encouragement to all who are called of the Lord to minister to His people!" Never take your calling lightly or for granted. Let us heed the words of the Apostle Paul to Timothy: "study to show thyself approved unto God, a workman that need not be ashamed, rightly dividing the word of truth" (II Timothy 2:15). Let us not be a marred vessel that has to be returned to the potter after close examination, but let us be a vessel chosen and fitted for the Master's use!

Verse for the Week
"If a man therefore purge himself from these, he shall be a vessel unto honor, sanctified, and meet for the master's use, and prepared unto every good work" (II Timothy 2:21)

Thought for the Week
Footprints in the sands of time are not made by sitting down.

Is There No Balm in Gilead?

May 6, 1984

"For the hurt of the daughter of my people am I hurt; I am black; astonishment hath taken hold of me. Is there no balm in Gilead; is there no physician there? Why then is not the health of the daughter of my people recovered" **Jeremiah 8:21–22**

Jeremiah chapters eight through eleven are full of accusations. The point is that the accusation was not directed against heathen nations; rather it is hurled against the chosen of God.

God can see flowers if there are any. He can see them before they open their mystery and proclaim in fragrance their gospel; He knows where they are sown and planted. But He looked, and there was none. He expected, and was struck to the heart with disappointment. No man repented of his wickedness, saying, "What have I done?" There was no personal cross-examination. When men ceased to converse with God, they cease to ask Him for guidance and direction. When men cease to converse with God, they cease to pray!

If we would but open our eyes and face realities, we would have to admit that our day is no different from that of Jeremiah's. The people showed no shame; they did as they pleased with no regard or reverence for God and His commandments. Note verse 12, did anyone blush? Not a soul! "They were not at all ashamed, neither could they blush." They could not blush! They had lost the power of being ashamed. One may become so familiar with intemperance that self-control becomes lacking in their lives. One can do and act un- righteously to the extent that they do not feel condemned in their act and show no repentance. "Is there no balm in Gilead? Can the sin-sick soul be healed? Is there no physician there? Why then is not the health of the daughter of my people recovered?"

The answer is yes; there is a balm in Gilead! Balm trees or plants grew in Gilead and were noted for their healing ingredients. The juice or sap from the trees was used to heal all wounds. The problem with Israel was that they would not take advantage of Gilead, which was not far from them. The Lord was not pleased with them for not heeding the man of God, Jeremiah.

Some may wonder what the relationship is between Jeremiah's day and the day in which we live. The man or woman of God preaches the gospel without compromise by telling people to heed their ways. Every man's ways are right in his own sight when he refuses or rejects the counsel of Jesus Christ. His word tells us that the wages of sin is death, but the gift of God is eternal life.

The church is faced with a deluge of divorces, unwed mothers, discontentment, murmuring, complaining, drunkenness, illicit sex, lazy men who do not want to work, men who do not want to take care of their families, and there is a great "falling away." Only because the people who say that they are the chosen of God refuse to look to Jesus Christ, the balm, for their healing! Yes, there is a balm in Gilead! It is not in the counselors, and I thank God for the knowledge they have concerning the problems we face. Jesus Christ is the balm we need! He is the ointment that can heal our wounds! If we would but look unto the hills from whence cometh our help, we would be a healthier, happier, and more spiritual family of God!

There is a balm in Gilead, for Jesus Christ said, "Because I live, ye shall live also. All power in heaven and earth is in my hand."

Verse for the Week
"But whoso looks into the perfect law of liberty and continues therein, he being not a forgetful hearer, but a doer of the work, this man shall be blessed in his deed" (James 1:25).

Thought for the Week
Salvation depends upon Christ's work for us, while rewards depend upon our works for Christ.

Love in Action

July 29, 1984

"Blessed are the meek: for they shall inherit the earth"
Matthew 5:5

There have been considerable differences of opinion as to the precise significance of the word *meek*. Some regard it as meaning patience, a spirit of resignation; some as unselfishness; others as gentleness, a spirit of no retaliation, bearing afflictions without complaint.

The first time the word *meek* appears in the scriptures is in Numbers 12:3. There we read of Miriam and Aaron speaking against Moses: "Hath the Lord indeed spoken only by Moses? Hath he not spoken also by us?" Such language betrayed the pride and haughtiness of their hearts, their self-seeking and looking for recognition. Moses was humble, lowly, and self-renouncing. He turned his back on worldly honors and earthly riches, choosing rather to suffer afflictions with the people of God (Hebrews 11:24–26).

Every saint who has the spirit of God should show love and compassion toward one another. The Bible admonishes us, "Brethren, if a man be overtaken in a fault, you which are spiritual, restore such an one in the spirit of meekness, considering thyself, lest you also be tempted" (Galatians 6:1). This demonstrates humility and lowliness. Sometimes man wants to direct God's plan of salvation according to his own thoughts. He is bent on making his own rules and laws. He charts his course to lead himself toward salvation and uses the Word of God to fit his concepts. God's ways are not our ways, but our ways must be God's ways! One who is meek and humble will follow God, not try to lead Him. Jesus said, "I am the way."

True meekness is not weakness. The apostles had been wrongfully beaten and cast into prison. On the following day the magistrates gave orders for their release, but Paul said to the keepers of the jail, "Let them come themselves and fetch us out." God-given meekness can stand up for God-given rights! The meek are those who have the greatest enjoyment of the things of this present life, those who have been delivered from a greedy and grasping spirit and are content with such things as they have.

The proud and restless do not inherit the earth even though they may own many acres of it. "A little that a righteous man hath is better than the riches of many wicked" (Psalms 37:16). The Lord Jesus Christ exemplified the spirit of meekness while on earth. Following His example, as meek men and women, we can, we are; we will be blessed! Let us put our love in action so all can see it and feel it.

Verse for the Week

"But the fruit of the spirit is love, joy, peace, long- suffering, gentleness, goodness, faith, meekness, temperance: against such there is no law" (Galatians 5:22–23).

Thought for the Week

The good that we do today becomes the happiness of tomorrow.

Jesus said, &Go, and Do Thou Likewise&

August 21, 1983

"Which now of these three, thinks thou, was neighbor unto him that fell among thieves? And he said, He that showed mercy on him. Then said Jesus unto him, go and do you likewise" Luke 10:36–37

This is a story that tells of the things that frequently happened on the way to Jerusalem on the Jericho Road. It was a road notoriously dangerous to travelers, a road of sharp turns and narrow defiles, a steep and narrow valley that provided excellent lurking places for bandits.

As we look at the characters in the story, we must note the traveler first. One thing stands out about him; he was either very careless or very reckless because seldom did any traveler venture on that road alone. Strangers were informed not to travel alone, but in a convoy, a group. Second, there was the priest who took one glance at the man laid there who had been attacked by a band of thieves and passed by on the other side. The Jews had all kinds of taboos. One was that anyone who touched a dead body was unclean for seven days (Numbers 19:11).

It is most likely that the priest was genuinely sorry for the wounded man, but he was not willing to investigate whether the man was dead.

If he was dead and the priest touched his body, he would automatically be shut out from functioning as a priest in the Temple for seven days. The priest set the Temple ritual above the needs of humanity.

Third, there was the Levite who apparently came over and looked at the man and then hurried past on the other side. There is one very probable explanation for this. It was a common thing for bandits to use a decoy; one of their members would act the part of a wounded man. Perhaps the Levite had this in mind: he would have liked to help, but the risk was too great. Then there was the Samaritan. The Jews did not like the Samaritans. The quarrel between them has lasted for 450 years. But the Good Samaritan had pity on the wounded man and did something about his needs. He not only bound the man's wounds and put him on his beast, but he took him not just to the inn, but to the innkeeper, and told the innkeeper to care for him, gave him what money he had with the assurance that if the money wasn't sufficient, he would pay the balance on his return.

Of all the parables of Jesus, this might be said to be the most practical. It deals with the most practical of all problems in the most practical way. It answers two questions: Who is my neighbor, and what is my duty to my neighbor in trouble? The answer is: Anyone who needs your help! Pity denotes action by helping or lending a helping hand. Jesus' words "Go and do likewise" are just as important and directed to us as when they were first uttered. The lesson is talking loud, and clear to every saint and Christian alike that if we say we want to be like Jesus, we must act like Him by not doing things that are only convenient or suitable for us.

The Lord Jesus Christ does not want us to be a respecter of person, nor are we to discriminate against a person's color, creed, or background; rather, we are to consider their need. "But whoso hath this world's goods and sees his brother have need, and shuttles up his bowels of compassion from him, how dwells the love of God in him" (I John 3:17)? May we be inspired to go and do likewise!

Verse for the Week

"And this commandment have we from Him, that he who loves God love his brother also" (I John 4:21).

Thought for the Week

There are so many ways we may make life count if we do all the good we can, in all the ways we can, as often as we can.

Salvation and the Love of God

June 14, 1978

"Therefore being justified by faith, we have peace with God through our Lord Jesus Christ: By whom also we have access by faith into this grace wherein we stand, and rejoice in hope of the glory of God" **Romans 5:1–2**

The understanding word is "peace." We are no longer at war within ourselves. We have given up our ways. This peace comes with faith. Salvation is deliverance from sin. Amnesty (Romans 5:1) is telling us that we have come under amnesty, a parting from your offense.

Romans 5:3-5. And not only [so], but we glory in tribulations also: knowing that tribulation works patience; and patience, experience; and experience, hope: And hope makes not ashamed; because the love of God is shed abroad in our hearts by the Holy Ghost which is given unto us.

This shows our maturity, which means growth. Cross and crown go together; to overcome self is a cross. A crown is received after we win or overcome the cross. Lucifer, the massager, lost his position. We must leave our present state and grow in grace. Tribulation brings about grief and also glory in Christ. These things are working for our good to bring about peace.

Romans 5:6–8. For when we were yet without strength, in due time Christ died for the ungodly. For scarcely for a righteous man will one die: yet peradventure for a good man some would even dare to die. But God commends his love toward us, in that, while we were yet sinners, Christ died for us.

This shows God's love toward the church. Eternal security is a gift from God. John 3:16 said no one merits the favor of God. He died because of His love for us. His love comes in to restrain us to come out from the world. John 3:17 should be read in conjunction with John 3:16. Galatians 2:20–21 tells us not to take our salvation for granted. There is no seniority because we are all saved by the grace of God and work with Him.

Ephesians 5:25–27 gives instruction to the husband and wife and the love of God toward the church. The love of Christ is unconditional and incomparable (Romans 5:7–8).

Verse for the Week

"You men of Galilee, why stand you gazing up into heaven? This same Jesus, that is taken up from you into heaven, shall so come in like manner as you have seen him go into heaven" (Acts 1:11).

Thought for the Week

Let us strive to please the Lord and always acknowledge Him in all our ways.

Blessed are the feet of them who preach the gospel!

SECTION II

Bible Class Notes

***Unless noted, all messages are compiled from
The author's Bible Class notes***

CHAPTER 7

Faith

January 4, 1978

Elder Andrew Davis

"Stand upon thy feet: for I have appeared unto thee for this purpose, to make thee a minister and a witness both of these things which thou hast seen, and of those things in which I will appear unto thee" **Acts 26:14–18**

To preach means to give out, to give what you have. If you don't have Jesus, you preach about Jesus. Only a Holy Ghost– filled person can preach Jesus (Mark 11:24, Romans 5:1, 10:17, Habakkuk 2:4). The just shall live by faith in things passed; present, and in the future (Hebrews 10:38–39, Hebrews 11:3).

There are three aspects of faith:

Doctrine, body of belief (Romans 6:17–18; Jude 3; Titus 1:4)

Application of faith (James 2:14)

Saving faith, the attributes of faith (Hebrews 11:1–8; 32–34)

In Luke 7, Jesus testifies of John the Baptist and denounces unbelief. The kingdom of God is in you. You can't see it. It's joy, peace, the Holy Ghost. The effectual prayer: Prayer consists of thanksgiving, praise, confession, petition, and intercession. We pray to obtain power. A prayerful attitude changes things and is a mind stayed on God.

Three things are necessary for life salvation:

A well-nourished life, fellowship, teaching, and studying

Good witness life, your life telling the story

Concentrated life, prayer, fasting, and seeking God

"A friend loves at all times, and a brother is born for adversity" (Proverbs 17:17). Jonathan and David are an example of friendship.

Friendship displays admiration, thankfulness, helpfulness, support, mutual interest, and trust.

There are three kinds of love:

Philo, love for family

Agape, Holy Ghost love, God love

Eros, love between husband and wife, man and woman, fleshly love

Elder Andrew Davis,

Assistant Pastor

Liberty

May 27, 1981

Morgan Park Assembly Church

Man was created to be free; a state of holy bliss, no sin (Genesis 2). We are held accountable for what we do when we know God's word (Genesis 3). The method that destroyed sin also saved us, baptism in Jesus' name, repentance, and the Holy Ghost. The water that destroyed the people saved the Ark (Genesis 7; 8).

After the flood, men were to have their own government until the call of Abraham (Genesis 8:15–11:31). The age of law was developed later (Leviticus 25:8–13). They work for six years and did nothing the seventh year. At the end of the 49th year, everyone was to go free on the 50th year, which was the year of Jubilee. In 586 BC, Israel, Judah, ceased to be a nation because they destroyed the Sabbath. In 1948 AD, they finally had a nation.

"Blessed are they which do hunger and thirst after righteousness: for they shall be filled. Blessed are the merciful: for they shall obtain mercy" (Matthew 5:6–7). The government today is called the kingdom of God. The citizens, saints, are given freedom by these laws. There is still another Jubilee to come called the New Heaven and the New Earth. No sin; No night (Revelation 21) A Sabbath of 700 years into eternity.

The church is God's government on the earth and the head is Jesus. Ananias and Sapphira tried to join the church with lies and brought forth death (Acts 5). Jesus tried to let the Jews know that they were in bondage of sin, but the Son could make them free (John 8:31–36). The unsaved see Jesus only as the Son of God. The saved see Jesus as the Father and we are the sons. Jesus came to release the captives (Luke 4:18–19).

Joy

July 15, 1981

Philippians 1–4

"Fulfill you my joy that you be like minded, having the same love being of one accord, of one mind" **Philippians 2:2**

We are to do things without murmurings and disputing. Hold fast to the word of God so you can rejoice in the day of Christ.

Paul admonishes us to stand fast in one spirit, with one mind, striving together for the faith of the gospel. Beware of false teaching. The Christian life goal should be to rejoice in the Lord.

We should never let circumstances, people, and things worry or rob us of our joy because joy is a wonderful feeling. Circumstances are our surroundings; we must deal with other's behavior, communication and the things that possess us. When worrying, you are unable to pray or go to church. You are not satisfied until you obtain things– money, clothes, cars, houses, and jobs. Worry centers on will the sun shine, will it rain and you are overwhelmed by the small things.

We can keep our joy provided we have a single mind, a submissive mind, a spiritual mind, and a secure mind.

The single mind: Philippians 1:19–21, Paul praised God for everything. He focused on salvation and let the world know, he was a prisoner of Christ only. James 1:8, a double mind is unstable.

The submissive mind: Philippians 2:1–3, Paul said we are to do nothing through strife or vainglory and we are to esteem each other.

The spiritual mind: Philippians 3:19–20, Paul said you are to look beyond the things you want and don't need.

The secure mind: Peace of God is ours when we practice it.

Right praying (Philippians 4:6–7)

Right thinking (Philippians 4:8)

Right living (Philippians 4:9)

Philippians 3:17–21: In these scriptures, Paul admonishes us to walk with a heavenly vision, a secure mind and peace with God.

Paul made it clear that we are not to have confidence in the flesh. He said, "What things were gain to me, I counted lost to Christ" (Philippians

3:3, 7). Things must be considered dung to win Christ. Our conversation should be in heaven because God supplies all our need. We need to rejoice in His righteousness.

Colossians 3:1–25

The Six Duties

January 14, 1981

"If you then be risen; with Christ, seek those things which are above, where Christ sits on the right hand of God"
Colossians 3:1

The third chapter of Colossians tells us what to seek and where to center our affections. It also tells us what to mortify and what to put on. Colossians lets us know that we have six duties which are:

Duty to new life interest (Colossians 3:1–4). Anyone who has a new life leaves the old one behind, spiritual and natural. When you are dead with Christ, you seek and set your affection on things above not, on things on the earth.

Duty to old life (Colossians 3:5–9). You are to mortify, kill, become dead; to anything that displeases God.

Uncleanness, impurity, and voracity

Inordinate affection, evil passion, and lusting

Covetousness, evil desire, and idolatry

Duty to new life (Colossians 3:10–15). If you have a new life, you are a new man. Your mind/ knowledge will be after the image of God. You will put on:

Bowels of mercies, compassion

Humbleness of mind, humility

Meekness, gentleness one toward another

Forbearing, putting up with one another,

understanding as much as possible.

Duty to the Church (Colossians 3:16–17). As part of God's church, the word of God will dwell in you. And whatsoever you do indeed, action, do it in the name of Christ.

Duty to domestic life (Colossians 3:18–21). This is to the believers. Wives are to submit themselves to their husbands as it is fit in the Lord. Husbands are to love their wives like Christ loves the church. Children must obey their parents in all things. Fathers should not discourage their children by provoking them to anger. A family must obey God's commandments to please him.

Duty to business life (Colossians 3:22–25). We are servants and must obey our master in the flesh, fearing God. We must do everything as to the Lord. Our reward will come from God. Servants are employees and masters are employers.

<u>*The Riches of Grace We Have in Christ Jesus*</u>

January 28, 1981

We don't need anyone to intercede for us. We can come to God boldly. Calvary brought salvation. God is long- suffering. He forgives every time we ask.

Background Scriptures:

Presence of God (Exodus 33:14)

The opportunity to come boldly to God's throne (Hebrews 4:16)

God's presence (II Corinthians 12:9)

Redemption, to be brought back (Ephesians 1:7)

Riches of His goodness (Romans 2:4)

The unmerited favor of God is grace. The following are words of expression to help us get a glimpse of God's grace.

Justified by faith, peace (Romans 5:1–2)

God supplying all our needs (Philippians 4:19) Salvation (Ephesians 2:8)

Kindness toward us (Ephesians 2:7)

Power to become the sons of God, the plan of salvation through Jesus (John 1:12–14)

Everlasting life (Galatians 6:7–9) Sonship, Son of God (Galatians 4:7–8) We are set free (Galatians 5:1)

We are redeemed and sanctified with wisdom and righteousness through Christ (I Corinthians 1:30–31)

Redemption through Christ's blood (Colossians 1:14)

Saved by grace, salvation raised up to heavenly places. This can be so here on earth because we are in Christ (Ephesians 2:5–6)

God's immutable promise for a strong consolation (Hebrews 6:13–18) Power to be witnesses (Acts 1:8)

Fellow citizens with saints and of the household of God (Ephesians 2:19) Do good to all men, but especially the household of faith (Galatians 6:10) All things work together for good to them that love God (Romans 8:28–29)

Grace was predestinated for us before our time and while we are in the world. We are in Christ and Christ in us (John 14:20)

We are a member of Christ's body (I Corinthians 12:13)

We are branches connected to the body of Christ (John 15:5) A stone in the building fitly joined together (Ephesians 2:19) All parts of the body are important.

We are sheep in the fold of God, no longer goats (John 10:27–29)

We are the bride of Christ. He wants His bride spotless (Ephesians 5:25–27) We are light in the Lord, no longer in darkness (Ephesians 5:8)

We have the right to possess every spiritual blessing of God (Ephesians 1:3)

<u>*Victory*</u>

August 19, 1981

The Holy Ghost is to help us live a victorious life every day. We are to live His word. We must line up with the word of God. Eat His word like you do fish, separate meat from bone.

Romans

6:1–14. 6:1.What shall we say then? Shall we continue in sin, that grace may abound?

6:2. God forbid. How shall we, that are dead to sin, live any longer therein?

6:3. Know you not, that so many of us as were baptized into Jesus Christ were baptized into his death?

6:4. Therefore we are buried with him by baptism into death: that like as Christ was raised up from the dead by the glory of the Father, even so we also should walk in newness of life.

6:5. for if we have been planted together in the likeness of his death, we shall be also in the likeness of his resurrection:

6:6. Knowing this, that our old man is crucified with him, that the body of sin might be destroyed, that henceforth we should not serve sin.

6:7. for he that is dead is freed from sin.

6:8. Now if we be dead with Christ, we believe that we shall also live with him:

6:9. Knowing that Christ being raised from the dead; dies no more, death hath no more dominion over him.

6:10 for in that he died, he died unto sin once: but in that he lives, he lives unto God.

6:11 likewise reckon you also yourselves to be dead indeed unto sin; but alive unto God through Jesus Christ our Lord.

6:12 let not sin therefore reign in your mortal body, that you should obey it in the lusts thereof.

6:13Neither yield you your members as instruments of unrighteousness unto sin: but yield yourselves unto God, as those that are alive from the dead, and your members as instruments of righteousness unto God.

6:14.For sin shall not have dominion over you: for you are not under the law, but under grace.

There are three deaths:

Dead to sin (Romans 6:11)

Dead to the law (Romans 7:4)

Dead to the flesh (Romans 8:13–14)

Your test comes from the save and the unsaved, but in the name of Jesus, we have the victory. To have a victorious life, we must:

Know (Romans 6:6)

Reckon, consider, accept, believe, immune to all things, dead (Romans 6:11)

Yield, being obedient (Romans 6:13)

Holiness is the order of the day no matter where we are. Yielding with obedience our:

Mind (Philippians 2)

Eyes (Job 31:1)

Ears (Mark 4:24)

Tongue (James 1:19; 3:1–10)

Hands (Proverbs 6:17)

Feet (Proverbs 6:18)

Vessel, body, the whole man (I Thessalonians 4:3–4)

CHAPTER 8

<u>**Focus Thought**</u>

A. Christian cults

Cults

February 11, 1981

B. Occults, Satan worshippers

1. Hinduism
2. Buddhism
3. Muslim

Christian cults are groups of people with knowledge of the Bible, but who strays away from its teachings while using it to establish their position.

Occults are not concerned with any form of religion but deal with witchcraft, Satan worshippers; mystics. You are initiated into the sect and sometimes murder is involved.

Background scriptures:

Matthew 7:15–20 tells us to beware of false prophets.

Matthew 24:4–5 says let no man deceive you.

Matthew 24:11, 24 speaks: of false Christ and prophets.

Thessalonians 2:10–11 talks about the power of Antichrist and strong delusion.

Timothy 4:1 says: some shall depart from the faith speaking openly.

The Difference Between Men and Angels

April 29, 1981

Angels are superior because man is made a little lower.

Psalm 8:4–6. When I consider thy heavens, the work of thy fingers, the moon and the stars, which thou hast ordained;

III Timothy 3:13–14 lets us know that false teaching is going to get worse. II Timothy 4:1–4 says our ears are turned away from the faith.

Jehovah Witness says only 144,000 are going to heaven.

We also have Mormonism, Christian Science, Seventh

Day Adventist, and Spiritualist.

A Church of God in Kentucky believes in snake worshipping. II John 10–11 tells what to do with Antichrist.

False teachers should not be entertained and never bid God speed, or encouraged in their ways.

<u>Noah and Family as Related to the Church</u>

September 9, 1981

NOAH

Noah had one wife.

1. A covenant was made 120 years before the flood (Genesis 6:16–19). They were chosen.
2. Noah called (Genesis 7:1)
3. Noah believed (Genesis 7:4–7).
4. Noah separated (Genesis 7:7).
5. God sealed the family from danger (Genesis 7:16).
6. Ark risen (Genesis 7:17–19)
7. They were rewarded with new things (Genesis 8:15-19.

CHURCH

Christ has one wife.

1. We are chosen before the foundation of the world (Ephesians 1:4).
2. Saints called (Romans 8:28–30; I Corinthians 1:9)
3. We believe (Hebrews 10:37–39).
4. Saints separated (John 17:13–20; I Peter 2:9)
5. Saints sealed by the Holy Ghost (Ephesians 1:13; 4:30).
6. Saints risen in Christ above the cares of this world (Colossians 3:1-4).
7. The saints were rewarded with a new heaven and a new earth.(Isaiah 65:17-25).

The Difference between Men and Angels

April 29, 1981

Angels are superior because man is made a little lower.

Psalm 8:4–6. When I consider thy heavens, the work of thy fingers, the moon and the stars, which thou hast ordained;

What is man, that thou art mindful of him? And the son of man, that thou visit him?

For thou has made him a little lower than the angels, and has crowned him with glory and honor.

Angels are spiritual beings.

Hebrews

6:1–14. Therefore leaving the principles of the doctrine of Christ, let us go on unto perfection; not laying again the foundation of repentance from dead works, and of faith toward God,

6:2.Of the doctrine of baptisms, and of laying on of hands; and of resurrection of the dead, and of eternal judgment.

6:3.And this will we do, if God permit.

6:4.For [it is] impossible for those who were once enlightened, and have tasted of the heavenly gift, and were made partakers of the Holy Ghost,

6:5.And have tasted the good word of God, and the powers of the world to come,

6:6. If they shall fall away, to renew them again unto repentance; seeing they crucify to themselves the Son of God afresh, and put him to an open shame.

6:7.For the earth which drinks in the rain that comes oft upon it, and bring forth herbs meet for them by whom it is dressed, receives blessing from God:

6:8. But that which bears thorns and briers is rejected, and is nigh unto cursing; whose end is to be burned.

6:9. But, beloved, we are persuaded better things of you, and things that accompany salvation, though we thus speak.

6:10. For God is not unrighteous to forget your work and labor of love, which you have showed toward his name, in that you have ministered to the saints, and do minister.

6:11.And we desire that every one of you do show the same diligence to the full assurance of hope unto the end:

6:12.That you be not slothful, but followers of them who through faith and patience inherit the promises.

6:13.For when God made promise to Abraham, because he could swear by no greater, he swore by himself,

6:14. Saying, Surely blessing I will bless you, and multiplying I will multiply you.

Luke 20:34–36. And Jesus answering said unto them, the children of this world marry, and are given in marriage:

20:35.But they which shall be accounted worthy to obtain the world; and the resurrection from the dead, neither marry, nor are given in marriage:

20:36.Neither can they die any more: for they are equal unto the angels; and are the children of God, being the children of the resurrection.

Angels don't marry.

Matthew 30

Angels are stronger in strength and intelligence. They don't get tired.

II Peter 2:11. Whereas angels, which are greater in power and might; bring not railing accusation against them before the Lord.

Angels are not redeemed by Jesus' blood; they are created holy.

I Peter 1:12. Unto whom it was revealed, that not unto themselves, but unto us they did minister the things, which are now reported unto you by them that have preached the gospel unto you with the Holy Ghost sent down from heaven; which things the angels desire to look into.

Angels are reapers.

Matthew 13:30. Let both grow together until the harvest: and in the time of harvest I will say to the reapers, gather you together first the tares (weeds), and bind them in bundles to burn them: but gather the wheat into my barn.

40–41.As therefore the tares are gathered and burned in the fire; so shall it be in the end of this world.

13:41. The Son of man shall send forth his angels, and they shall gather out of his kingdom all things that offend, and them which do iniquity;

Saints judge angels.

I Corinthians 6:3. Know ye not that we shall judge angels? How much more things that pertain to this life?

Men are appointed to die.

Hebrews 9:27. And as it is appointed unto men once to die: but after this the judgment:

Angels' job is in heaven and men's job is on earth.

Thessalonians 1:7–10

1:7.And to you who are troubled rest with us, when the Lord Jesus shall be revealed from heaven: with his mighty angels.

1:8. In flaming fire taking vengeance on them that know not God: and that obey not the gospel of our Lord Jesus Christ:

1:9.Who shall be punished with everlasting destruction from the presence of the Lord, and from the glory of his power;

1:10.When he shall come to be glorified in his saints; and to be admired in all them that believe (because our testimony among you was believed) in that day.

What do men and angels have in common?

Luke 15:10. They rejoice when sinners are found.

After the first part of chapter seven of Revelation, the church is gone.

The Names of Satan

May 6 and 13, 1981

Lucifer was an angel of God who wanted to be like God. His favorite word was "I." He deceived Eve in the Garden of Eden. Because this was the first lie, he became the father of lies. He introduced Eve to lust of the flesh, lust of the eye, and the pride of life (I John 2:15–17). These three led Eve to entice her husband to disobey God's commandment, which brought about our sinful nature.

As part of Lucifer's curse, he received the name Satan along with the following:

Angel of the Bottomless Pit (Revelation 9:11). Abaddom (Hebrew) or Apollyon (Greek) means "destroyer."

Dragon, serpent, devil, Satan (Revelation 20:3). Devil comes from *diabolus*, which means "slander." Dragon means to trap, fool people.

Leviathan, serpent, dragon (Isaiah 27:1)

Liar, murderer (John 8:44)

Beelzebub (Matthew 12:24). Serpent denotes cunning, sneaky, sly, and crafty.

Prince of this World (John 16:11). World means the "system."

Prince of Power of the Air (Ephesians 2:2). Air means the "outer area."

Prince of the Kingdom of Persia (Daniel 10:13)

Tempter, to entice (Matthew 4:3)

God of this world (II Corinthians 4:4)

Lucifer, messenger of light. His desire denotes darkness; he fell from his state and lost the name Lucifer

Belial (II Corinthians 6:14–16)

Wicked one (I John 5:18).

Adversary (I Peter 5:6–9)

Little horn (Daniel 7:8)

Canon, fox, wolf (II Corinthians 11:11–15), transformed into an angel of light and minister of righteousness

Antichrist (I John 2:18–22)

Ruler of Darkness, king (Ephesians 6:12)

Thorn in the Flesh (II Corinthians 12:7)

<u>What Defense Do We Have against Satan?</u>

May 13, 1981

Naturally, we have no defense against Satan. Satan is not afraid of man. We must fast and keep a prayerful life to be spiritually ready to fight Satan with the sword. The sword is the word of God. The word provides us with the weapon we need to defend ourselves.

Along with God's word, we have the following:

Name of Jesus (Acts 16:17–18, Colossians 3:17)

God's authority (Ephesians 4:26–27)

The whole armor, the truth (Ephesians 6:11–18), the shield of faith, the helmet of salvation, the sword of the spirit, prayer of supplication.

The blood of the Lamb and the Saint's testimony (Revelation 12:10– 11)

The name of Jesus to get our authority (Mark 6:15–18)

The fear of the Lord's name (Isaiah 59:19)

Prayer and thinking right (Philippians 4:6–8)

The Lord is not slack with His promises (II Peter 3:9)

All God's promises are true and not slack (Colossians 1:20)

Angels: Messengers of God

October 15, 1975

Throughout the Bible, angels are the ones God sends to speak to us. I'm going to mention five incidents.

It was an angel that visited Abraham and Sarah telling them about the future birth of Isaac (Genesis 15–18).

Two angels visited Lot before Sodom and Gomorrah were destroyed (Genesis 19).

It was an angel, Gabriel, who visited Zacharias telling him about the conception, birth, and name of John the Baptist (Luke 1).

It was Gabriel who spoke to Mary about being pregnant with Jesus and spoke to Joseph her husband to be (Luke 1).

It was angels who foretold the birth of Jesus to the shepherds (Luke 2).

Background Scriptures:

Jesus teaches angels (Matthew 13:36–43; 18:7–10). Angels are created (Colossians 1:16).

Creation praises the Lord (Psalms 148:1–5).

Michael, the angel, interprets Daniel's vision (Daniel 10:10–13). The angels named in the Bible are Gabriel and Michael (Jude 9). Gabriel, the messenger, announced Jesus' birth (Luke 1:12–26).

The Lord gives His angels charge over thee to keep thee in all thy ways. Angels are sent to minister to us (Hebrews 1:7–12).

Satan transforms himself into an angel of the light and his false minister (II Corinthians 11:12–17).

Three Important Things in a Saint's Life

February 18, 19, 1981

Saints should always have:
A regular prayer life
A regular Bible-reading life
A regular witnessing life

Prayer Life

I Thessalonians 5:15–17. Prayer is the way we communicate with God.

David and the three Hebrew boys are good examples of a prayerful life. When you pray, you store up treasure in heaven that you can use in time of trouble.

Bible-reading Life

I Timothy 4:11–14. The Bible teaches us to study to show ourselves approved. You can't teach what you don't know.

Witnessing Life

Acts1:8, 8:26–35, John 8:1–11. You must read the word of God to know His commandments. Your life at home, on your job, wherever you go, should be a witness for Christ.

Prayer, the word of God, the Bible, and witnessing to others is the way we communicate to God and He to us.

Background Scriptures:

Galatians 5:22–23. Patience, fruit of the spirit and exercise self-control
I Corinthians 40:1. Faithfulness

Romans 12:1–2. Your reasonable service

Adversity

June 10, 1981

Adversity is conflict, test, problem, opposition, trials, and trouble. The Holy Ghost will help you through adversity. God gives rest for the soul (Matthew 11:28–30).

Adversity is easier to endure and overcome when you are a child of God. All things work together for good.

Romans 8:28–29. And we know that all things work together for good to them that love God, to them who are the called according to his purpose.

8:29.For whom he did foreknow, he also did predestinate to be conformed to the image of his Son, that he might be the firstborn among many brethren when we stray, God chastens us as sons.

Hebrews 12:6. For whom the Lord loves he chasten, and scourge every son whom he receives.

12:7. If you endure chastening: God deals with you as with sons: for what son is he whom the father chasten not?

12:10.For they verily for a few days chastened us: after their own pleasure; but he for our profit, that we might be partakers of his holiness.

12:11. Now no chastening for the present seems to be joyous, but grievous: nevertheless afterward it yields the peaceable fruit of righteousness unto them which are exercised thereby.

Our accountability is to God. Fear and knowledge are wisdom and understanding.

Background Scriptures:

Judges2:20. And the anger of the LORD was hot against Israel; and he said, because, this, people has transgressed my covenant: which I commanded their fathers, and have not hearkened unto my voice;

2:21. I also will not henceforth drive out any from before them of the nations which Joshua left when he died:

2:22.That through them I may prove Israel, whether they will keep the way of the LORD to walk therein, as their fathers did keep it, or not.

Ephesians 6:10. Finally, my brethren, be strong in the Lord, and in the power of his might.

6:11. Put on the whole armor of God; that you may be able to stand against the wiles of the devil.

6:12.For we wrestle not against flesh and blood, but against principalities, against powers, against the rulers of the darkness of this world, against spiritual wickedness in high places.

6:13.Wherefore, take unto you the whole armor of God: that ye may be able to withstand in the evil day, and having done all, to stand.

6:14. Stand therefore, having your loins girt about with truth, and having on the breastplate of righteousness;

6:15.And your feet shod with the preparation of the gospel of peace;

6:16. Above all taking the shield of faith; wherewith ye shall be able to quench all the fiery darts of the wicked.

6:17And take the helmet of salvation, and the sword of the Spirit, which is the word of God:

6:18.Praying always with all prayer and supplication in the Spirit, and watching thereunto with all perseverance and supplication for all saints;

Four Basic structures of Authority

July 20, 1977

"The eyes of the LORD are in every place, beholding the evil and the good" (Proverbs 15:3).

Our society deals with the family, the government, the church, and the business; the saints are governed by all four.

The Family

Colossians 3:20–21. A good family (Ephesians 6:1–4: Proverbs 6:20–21, 30:17). Proverbs 15:5. Children are to obey and honor their parents, to be prudent. Fathers are not to provoke their children to wrath and discouragement; teach the children the way of the Lord. The wives are to submit and the husbands are to love them like Christ loves us, the church.

The Government

I Peter 2:11–15, Romans 13:1–7. God wants us to abstain from fleshly lust, to have honest conversation, and to submit to the ordinance of man. When we do well, we put to silence the ignorance of foolish men. We are to do everything as unto the Lord.

The Church

I Thessalonians 5:11–13. We are to comfort, edify, and esteem one another with the thought of being rapture one day.

The Business

Colossians 3:22–24, I Peter 2:18, I Timothy 6:1–2. The Bible speaks of a servant and a master as being brethren. Each of them must show honor and be faithful.

Evidence of Salvation and Deliverance

January 11, 1978

"Therefore if any man be in Christ, he is a new creature: old things are passed away; behold all things are become new" (II Corinthians 5:17).

Webster's says evidence is to make clear. It tends to prove your statement. Therefore, when anyone makes a claim of salvation or deliverance, he or she must produce evidence.

The evidence I'm speaking of must be all of the following:

Spiritual life: New awareness of right and wrong

Spiritual food: Hunger for God's word (Romans 10:9–10), confirming salvation

Spiritual growth: Desire for a changed life

Testing of faith: Increase in testing

Fellowship: Love for other Christians

Witness: Desire to tell others about Christ (Romans 6:4), buried with Jesus by baptism into death.

Spiritual life: Beware of right and wrong (John 16:7–11, Romans 7:18–25), in my flesh dwells no good thing.

Spiritual food (Job 23:12, Jeremiah 15:16), eat God's word.

New creature (II Corinthians 5:17).

Blessed are ye when men hate you (Luke 6:22).

Fellowship, love one another (I John 4:7–13).

Witnessing, let the redeemed of the Lord say so (Psalms 107:2).

CHAPTER 9

<u>Focus Thought</u>

<u>*Moral impurity*</u>

June 4, 1980

"Dearly beloved, I beseech you as strangers and pilgrims, abstain from fleshly lusts, which war against the soul" (I Peter 2:11).

Holy is what God called us for; therefore, we must be clean. After the Holy Ghost, some of us get dirty, impure, and unclean. The Holy Ghost protects us from the dirt. Self is a great issue. Lasciviousness means unbridled passion (Galatians 5:17–19). Passion does not always mean sex; it can be money.

We are to beware of false doctrines and pernicious, sneaky, destructive, and selfless people having no control over their actions. No saint should be destructive (II Peter 2:1–2).

Wantonness is greed and overanxious (II Peter 2:18).

We are admonished to know or learn how to control ourselves to avoid concupiscence, a strong desire to satisfy the sexual appetite. Be careful of what we say because we don't want to arouse the lust of the flesh (I Thessalonians 4:4–5).

Romans 6:12 tells us about lust and Romans 7:7 tells us about covet. Moral impurity is unclean. Defraud is dishonest (I Corinthians 7:5, Mark 10:19).

Moral impurity and all it entails can be—and is— dangerous. The end result is God giving you up to a reprobate mind. A reprobate is a person who has rejected God and believes a lie and not the truth (Romans 1:21–28, Romans 6:12).

<u>Christian Conduct</u>

November 6, 1975

"Murmuring is a problem and causes our conduct not to be what it should be and someone is affected by it". How our conduct affects others (Romans 14:7– 8).

We should ask ourselves three questions to make sure our conduct is in line with God.

Does our conduct offend others?

Is our behavior a good example?

Does it please God?

Christians are to be Christ-like with the following:

Family Behavior

Titus 2:1–15. We are to teach and honor one another. Observe the doctrine of God while looking for the arrival of Jesus.

How We Must Walk

Ephesians 4:1–3. We must walk worthy in love and unite.

Stand True to Your Faith

Philippians 1:27–28. Even in suffering, we must stand true for God and be a good example to others (I Timothy 4:11–12).

<u>Hindrances to Our Walk with God</u>

July 21, 1982

Anyone who feels a little off key, not knowing where he should be in the Lord, needs to evaluate what's going on in his or her life. The list below is a beginning. Sometimes we are in the church but don't realize that we are really outside looking in. We are there, but distant. We make excuses as to why we are not participating in any of the auxiliaries.

Snow White and the Seven Dwarfs

Isaiah 1:18. Come now, and let us reason together, says the LORD: though your sins be as scarlet, they shall be as white as snow; though they be red like crimson, they shall be as wool.

1:19 If you be willing and obedient, you will eat the good of the land:

There are seven deadly sins:

1. Pride (Proverbs 16:18; 29:23; 6:16–19)

Greed (avarice) (Ecclesiastes 4:7–8)

Envy (jealousy) (Proverbs 14:30, Galatians 5:26, Solomon 8:6, Philippians 2:3)

Lust (Galatians 5:16)

Wrath (Ephesians 4:26)

Hatred (I John 2:9-11)

Sloth (Romans 12:11)

Are you paying tithes? Have you ever paid tithes? Have you lost sight of your spiritual values and love of worship and praise to God?

Together

March 4 and 11, 1981

The foundation of God begins with love.

I Corinthians 13:2. And though I have the gift of prophecy, and understand all mysteries, and all knowledge; and though I have all faith, so that I could remove mountains, and have not charity, I am nothing.

13:3.And though I bestow all my goods to feed the poor, and though I give my body to be burned, and have not charity, it profits me nothing.

13:4. Charity suffers long, and is kind; charity envies not; charity vaunt (boast) not itself is not puffed up,

13:8. Charity never fails: but whether there be prophecies, they shall fail; whether there be tongues, they shall cease; whether there be knowledge, it shall vanish away.

I John 4:11. Beloved, if God so loved us, we ought also to love one another

3:18.My little children, let us not love in words, or in tongue; but in deed and in truth.

A Christian deed and action!

Romans 12:3–5. For I say, through the grace given unto me, to every man that is among you, not to think of himself more highly than he ought to think; but to think soberly, according as God has dealt to every man the measure of faith.

12:4.For as we have many members in one body, and all members have not the same office:

12:5.So we, being many, are one body in Christ, and every one member's one of another.

I Corinthians 12:14. For the body is not one member, but many.

12:15. If the foot shall say, because I am not the hand, I am not of the body; is it therefore not of the body?

12:16.And if the ear shall say, because I am not the eye, I am not of the body; is it therefore not of the body?

12:17.If the whole body were an eye, where were the hearing? If the whole were hearing, where is the smelling?

12:25.That there should be no schism in the body; but that the members should have the same care one for another.

12:26.And whether one member suffers, all the members suffer with it; or one member be honored, all the members rejoice with it.

Schism is separation or division.

Romans 12:9–10. Let love be without dissimulation. Abhor that which is evil; cleave to that which is good.

12:10.Be kindly affectionate one to another with brotherly love; in honor preferring one another;

Devoted to each other

Ephesians 4:32. And be you kind one to another, tenderhearted, forgiving one another, even as God for Christ's sake has forgiven you.

Harmony

Romans 15:5. Now the God of patience and consolation grant you to be likeminded one toward another according to Christ Jesus:

15:6.That you may with one mind and one mouth glorify God, even the Father of our Lord Jesus Christ.

15:7.Wherefore receive you one another, as Christ also received us to the glory of God.

Dissimulation, false pretense, deceitfulness

Romans 12:16. Be of the same mind one toward another. Mind not high things, but condescend to men of low estate. Be not wise in your own conceits.

John 17:14–21. I have given them your word; and the world has hated them, because they are not of the world, even as I am not of the world.

17:15. I pray not that you should take them out of the world, but that you should keep them from the evil.

17:16They are not of the world, even as I am not of the world. 17:17. Sanctify them through your truth: your word is truth.

17:18.As you have sent me into the world, even so have I also sent them into the world.

17:19.And for their sakes I sanctify myself, that they also might be sanctified through the truth.

17:20. I do not pray for these alone, but for them also which shall believe on me through their word;

17:21.That they all may be one; as you, Father, are in me, and I in you, that they also may be one in us: that the world may believe that you have sent me.

Serve one another

Galatians 5:13. For, brethren, you have been called unto liberty; but don't use your liberty for an occasion to the flesh, but by love serve one another.

Bear one another's burdens

Galatians 6:2. Bear you one another's burdens, and so fulfill the law of Christ.

The strong are to bear the infirmity of the weak.

Romans 15:1–2. We then that are strong ought to bear the infirmities of the weak, and not to please ourselves.

15:2.Let every one of us please his neighbor for his good to edification.

Edify one another

I Thessalonians 5:11. Wherefore comfort yourselves together, and edify one another, even as also you do.

5:14.Now we exhort you, brethren, warn them that are unruly, comfort the feebleminded, support the weak; be patient toward all men.

Unity of the Spirit

Ephesians 4:3.Endeavoring to keep the unity of the Spirit in the bond of peace.

4:13.Till we all come in the unity of the faith, and of the knowledge of the Son of God, unto a perfect man, unto the measure of the stature of the fullness of Christ

<u>Three Days and Three Nights</u>

April 15, 1981

The Bible does not use our calendar, but the Jewish calendar.

Matthew 12:40. For as Jonas was three days and three nights in the whale's belly; so shall the Son of man be three days and three nights in the heart of the earth.

12:41.The men of Nineveh shall rise in judgment with this generation, and shall condemn it: because they repented at the preaching of Jonas; and, behold, a greater than Jonas [is] here.

The Passover began on the 14th day, Wednesday, when the sun went down.

The Jewish day began after 6 p.m.

Jesus was taken Wednesday, the 14/15. The 15th was a holiday for the Feast of Unleavened Bread. He was crucified on Wednesday and taken down by 3 p.m. and placed in the grave by or before 6 p.m. By our calendar, he would have been put in the grave on Thursday before 6 p.m., continue Friday and Saturday, and rose early Sunday morning.

<u>*Ten Miracles Performed by Jesus*</u>

June 24, 1981

Matthew 8 and 9

When Jesus walked on earth, healing the people of their infirmities, many believed and became Christian. However, the ruler sought to kill Him.

I have listed below the most favorable, outstanding miracles.

Jesus heals the leper (Matthew 8:1–4).

Centurion's servant healed (Matthew 8:5–13), palsy.

Peter's mother-in-law healed (Matthew 8:14– 15), fever.

Demons cast out; Mary healed (Matthew 8:16–17).

Jesus stills the storm (Matthew 8:23–27).

Maniacs of Gergesa herd of swine, two possessed with devil (Matthew 8:28–34).

Palsy man healed (Matthew 9:1–8).

Woman healed, issue of blood 12 years (Matthew 9:18–22).

Girl resurrected (Matthew 9:23–26).

Two blind men healed (Matthew 9:27–31).

Dumb man healed (Matthew 9:32–34).

The three functional diseases that affect the whole body:

Leprosy, sin

Palsy

Fever

Demons cast out, Jesus showing his matchless power.

Now there's Daniel, Gabriel battled with Satan 21 days. Michael came to help so he could give Daniel the answer he had been seeking about a vision (Daniel 10). Of course, there was Daniel in the lion's den and the three Hebrew boys.

Jesus& Teachings That Help and Encourage Us

June 17, 1981

Matthew 5–7

Jesus lets us know in these three chapters that the saints and His church are the earth's preservative, salt, and the earth's light to those in darkness. We have the responsibility to feed His sheep.

In **chapter five,** He emphasizes the terribleness of eternal hell. He speaks on unlawful relationships, love, blessing, doing, and prayer. He deals with:

The Beatitudes (Matthew 5:3–16)

Moral standards (Matthew 5:17–48)

Chapter six, Jesus teaches:

Religious motives (Matthew 6:1–18).

Mammon worship (Matthew 6:19–24), fame, riches, power, greed for wealth and fortune.

Temporal cares (Matthew 6:25–34), anxiety, lust, worry, and greed. He admonishes us to be charitable, Christ like. Giving does not always mean money. Give of yourself if that's all you have to give. Service lays up treasure in heaven. This enables you to concentrate fully on God and to help all men who need help.

Chapter seven deals with:

Social discernment (Matthew 7:1–6), good judgment and discretion.

Encouragement (Matthew 7:7–11).

Summary in a sentence (Matthew 7:12).

The alternatives (Matthew 7:13–14), choices.

The final warning (Matthew 7:15–27), false prophets. We are never to find fault with anyone except ourselves. When we ask God for anything, believe that it is done. Verse12 deals with judging, fault- finding, mote hunting, dispensing holy things, and parental responsibility. We are warned that the teaching of false prophets can lead to our destruction.

Christ&s Invitation

September 2, 1981

Matthew 11:28–30. Come unto me, all you that labor and are heavy laden, and I will give you rest.

11:29. Take my yoke upon you, and learn of me; for I am meek and lowly in heart: and you shall find rest unto your souls.

11:30.For my yoke is easy, and my burden is light.

Who are the invited?

He that hears (Revelation 22:17–18)

He that has an ear and over comes (Revelation 2:11)

God sends a famine, thirsting to hear His word (Amos 8:11, Matthew 5:6)

The good news is for everyone. God has no respect of person. But if you don't listen, you can't hear. The Bible says, he that has an ear to hear let him hear

Who will come?

The ones that God draws (John 6:44–45); Few will come. The gate is narrow because only a few will endure to the end. The reprobate mind individuals will not come.

What must one do to come?

Confess and believe (Romans 10:9–10).

In the beginning God:

Monotheism means one God.

Atheism means no God.

Polytheism means many gods.

In the beginning God created.

Fatalism is doctrine of chance.

Evolution is infinite becoming.

God created the heaven and the earth.

Pantheism makes God and the universe identical.

Materialism doctrine accepts the eternity of matter.

What will Christ do?

He will not leave us (John 6:37). He's coming back for those who have His name and have held on till the very end.

The Rapture

May 10, 1978

The Bible does not use the word rapture. The Bible talks about being caught up. Two examples:

"Enoch walked with God: and he was not for God took him" (Genesis 5:24). Then there was Elijah who was taken up into heaven by a whirlwind (II King 2).

The saints of God are waiting for the day of the Lord. The day He descends from heaven and those who are dead and alive will meet Him in the air. Let's not forget, Jesus was taken up, rapture, after His death. The Bible lets us know that we must be ready at all times so we can hear the trumpet. The mortal to immortal takes place when we are caught up to meet Christ in the air.

Background Scriptures:

I Thessalonians 4:13–18. But I would not have you to be ignorant, brethren, concerning them which are asleep, that you sorrow not, even as others which have no hope.

4:14. For if we believe that Jesus died and rose again, even so them also which sleep in Jesus will God bring with him.

4:15.For this we say unto you by the word of the Lord, that we which are alive and remain unto the coming of the Lord shall not prevent them which are asleep.

4:16. For the Lord himself shall descend from heaven with a shout, with the voice of the archangel, and with the trump of God: and the dead in Christ shall rise first:

4:17.Then we which are alive and remain shall be caught up together with them in the clouds, to meet the Lord in the air: and so shall we ever be with the Lord.

4:18.Wherefore, comfort one another with these words.

Acts 1:10–11. And while they looked steadfastly toward heaven as he went up, behold, two men stood by them in white apparel;

1:11.Which also said, you men of Galilee, why stand you gazing up into heaven? This same Jesus, which is taken up from you into heaven; shall so come in like manner as you have seen him go into heaven.

Mark 16:19. So then after the Lord had spoken unto them, he was received up into heaven, and sat on the right hand of God.

I John 3:1–3. Behold what manner of love the Father has bestowed upon us, that we should be called the sons of God: therefore the world knows us not, because it knew him not.

3:2. Beloved, now are we the sons of God, and it does not yet appear what we shall be: but we know that, when he shall appear, we shall be like him; for we shall see him as he is.

3:3.And every man that has this hope in him purifies himself, even as he is pure.

I Corinthians 15:51–58. Behold, I show you a mystery; we shall not all sleep, but we shall all be changed,

15:52. In a moment, in the twinkling of an eye, at the last trump: for the trumpet shall sound, and the dead shall be raised incorruptible, and we shall be changed.

15:53.For this corruptible must put on incorruption, and this mortal must put on immortality.

15:54.So when this corruptible put on incorruption, and this mortal put on immortality, then the saying that is written will come true; Death is swallowed up in victory.

15:55. O death, where is thy sting? O grave, where is thy victory? 15:56. The sting of death is sin; and the strength of sin is the law.

15:57.But thanks be to God, which gives us the victory through our Lord Jesus Christ.

15:58. Therefore, my beloved brethren, be you steadfast, unmovable, always abounding in the work of the Lord, forasmuch as you know that your labor is not in vain in the Lord.

Revelation 20:4–6. And I saw thrones, and they sat upon them, and judgment was given unto them: and I saw the souls of them that were beheaded for the witness of Jesus, and for the word of God, and which had not worshipped the beast, neither his image, neither had received his mark upon their foreheads, or in their hands; and they lived and reigned with Christ a thousand years.

20:5. But the rest of the dead lived not again until the thousand years were finished. This is the first resurrection.

20:6.Blessed and holy is he that has part in the first resurrection: on such the second death has no power, but they shall be priests of God and of Christ, and shall reign with him a thousand years.

Luke 17:31–36. In that day, he which shall be upon the housetop, and his stuff in the house, let him not come down to take it away: and he that is in the field, let him likewise not return back.

17:32. Remember Lot's wife.

17:33.Whosoever shall seek to save his life shall lose it; and whosoever shall lose his' life shall preserve it.

17:34. I tell you, in that night there shall be two men in one bed; the one shall be taken, and the other shall be left.

17:35.Two women shall be grinding together; the one shall be taken, and the other left.

17:36.Two men shall be in the field; the one shall be taken, and the other left.

17:37.And they answered and said unto him, Where, Lord? And he said unto them, where ever the body is; there will the eagles be gathered together.

Don&t Be a Lukewarm Christian

June 9, 1991

"I know your works, that you are neither cold nor hot; I would that you were cold or hot. So then because you are lukewarm and neither cold nor hot: I will spit you out of my mouth" (Revelation 3:15–16).

The church at Laodecia seemed to be more concerned about its material wealth than worshipping the Lord of glory. They prided themselves in three areas—*their financial wealth, their clothing trade, and their medical center,* which caused them to lose sight of their spiritual values and love of worship and praise to God.

Jesus was very troubled by these people— not the infidels, the atheist, or the person classified as an outrageous sinner, but the "church" people! He is speaking of the lukewarm, indifferent, and neglectful they characterized. Here is the harm in "being lukewarm"; as a member of the body of Christ, the Christian is representing Him. When the "world" notices the life that is lived is no different from them, they will conclude that there is nothing to being saved or religion is false.

Let us not be lukewarm when it comes to our Christian integrity. I'm sure that everyone in debt intends to pay back, although some may be a little slow in doing so. They don't intend to be dishonest but are somewhat neglectful in their intention of paying back the debt that is owed. We can learn from the Bible of what the Lord will have us do and we are to do it. He is our Savior and the Lord of our lives and we should be up and about our Father's business. We should read, obey, and live His word (the Bible)!

Let us ask ourselves: "Am I faithful? Am I lined up with the church of Christ? Do I put the Lord's house above every other institution?" Let us make up in our minds that we will not be like the church at Laodecia and take advantage in all that the church has to offer us spiritually— prayer services, Bible classes, Sunday school, and praise and worship services. Let us prove Him by bringing our tithes and offerings and doing all we can for the Lord.

As we are obedient to God, we will be in the position to hear Him say, "Well done, thou good and faithful servant."

Verse for the Week:
"Slothfulness casts into a deep sleep; and an idle soul shall suffer hunger" (Proverbs 19:15)

Thought for the Week:
Let us drown being lukewarm in the sea of God's forgetfulness.

SECTION III

Meditations for the Week

***Unless noted, all messages are compiled from the
author's precious keepsake journals***

Day and night

I will meditate on your Word.

CHAPTER 10

Scripture and Thoughts for the Month and Year

January

Scripture: And that, knowing the time, that now it is high time to awake out of sleep: for now is our salvation nearer than when we believed (Romans 13:11).

For our gospel came not unto you in word only, but also in power, and in the Holy Ghost, and in much assurance; as ye know what manner of men we were among you for your sake (I Thessalonians 1:5).

Thought: There are so many ways we may make life count if we do all the good we can, in all the ways we can, as often as we can.

The will of God will not lead where the grace of God cannot keep.

February

Scripture: Pure religion and undefiled before God and the Father is this, to visit the fatherless and widows in their afflictions, and to keep oneself unspotted from the world (James 1:27).

"And as it is appointed unto men once to die, but after this the Judgment" (Hebrews 9:27).

Thought: The Spirit of God enlightens our understanding as we read the word of God with a desire to do His will. Following the opinions of people instead of listening to God brings His judgment.

March

Scripture: Understanding is a wellspring of life unto him that hath it: but the instruction of fools is folly (Proverbs 16:22).

But God forbid that I should glory, save in the cross of our Lord Jesus Christ, by whom the world is crucified unto me, and I unto the world (Galatians 6:14).

Thought: No one will ever be disappointed with the final outcome when his life is in God's hands.

If men are to be saved from the power of sin, they must look to Christ, our only hope.

April

Scripture: Looking unto Jesus, the author and finisher of our faith, who for the joy that was set before him endured the cross, despising the shame, and is set down at the right hand of the throne of God (Hebrews 12:2).

Scripture: He staggered not at the promise of God through unbelief; but was strong in faith, giving glory to God; and being fully persuaded that, what he had promised, he was able to perform (Romans 4:20–21).

Thought: Christians without crosses are swords without blades.

God always provides what is necessary to meet our needs. Let us always be on guard against the danger of setting a limit on what Christ can do through us.

May

Scripture: God is greatly to be feared in the assembly of the saints, and to be had in reverence of all them; that are about him (Psalms 89:7).

That he would grant unto us, that we, being delivered out of the hand of our enemies, Might serve him without fear. In holiness and righteousness; before him, all the days of our life (Luke 1: 74–75)

Thought: All we are we are by God's grace in our Lord Jesus Christ.

Obedience to God's word is far more important than material gain. When we place Him first in our lives, He will add the material blessings that we need!

June

Scripture: Flee also youthful lusts: but follow righteousness, faith, charity, peace, with them that call on the Lord out of a pure heart (II Timothy 2:22).

But they that wait upon the Lord shall renew their strength; they shall mount up with wings as eagles; they shall run, and not be weary; and they shall walk, and not faint (Isaiah 40:31).

Keep my commandments, and live; and my law as the apple of your eye bind them upon your fingers, write them upon the table of your heart (Proverbs 7:2– 3).

Thought: Our love for the Lord is perfected only to the extent that we obey His word.

Daily we should pray, Heavenly Father, glorify your name through me.

Only the Spirit of God can prompt us to speak what will honor Him. The Spirit of God in our lives can prompt us to testify of His wonderful salvation.

July

Scripture: Let this mind be in you, which was also in Christ Jesus (Philippians 2:5).

Marvel not at this: for the hour is coming, in the which all that are in the graves shall hear his voice, And shall come forth; they that have done good, unto the resurrection of life; and they that have done evil, unto the resurrection of damnation (St. John 5:28–29).

Thought: Christ's resurrection is the assurance of victory over death for all who are saved.

The mind, body, and spirit of every saint, Christian, and follower of Christ should bring honor to a loving and Holy God.

August

Scripture: Let us draw near with a true heart in full assurance of faith, having our heart sprinkled from an evil conscience, and our bodies washed with pure water (Hebrews 10:22).

But the meek shall inherit the earth; and shall delight themselves in the abundance of peace (Psalms 37:11).

Thought: God desires that we rid ourselves of all unbelief and selfishness.

If we remember that the Lord is with us, we will not be defected by the afflictions of life.

September

Scripture: Thus says the LORD, your redeemer, the Holy One of Israel; I am the LORD your God which teaches you to profit, which leads you by the way that you should go (Isaiah 48:17).

Remember now your Creator in the days of your youth, while the evil days come not, nor the years draw nigh, when you shall say, I have no pleasures in them (Ecclesiastes 12:1).

Thought: We can trust our lives in the protective hands of our Almighty Father.

Teach a child to choose the right path and when he is older, he will remain upon it.

October

Scripture: Continue in prayer, and watch in the same with thanksgiving (Colossians 4:2).

Go your ways: behold, I send you forth as lambs among wolves (Luke 10:3).

Thought: Oh thou who hast given us so very much, grant us one thing more, a grateful heart.

Are you about your Father's business, doing His will?

Christ guides and strengthens His people at all times. Our responsibility is to acknowledge Him in all our ways.

November

Scripture: And he said unto them, Take heed, and beware of covetousness: for a man's life consists not in the abundance of the things that he possesses (Luke 12:15).

Giving thanks always for all things unto God and the Father in the name of our Lord Jesus Christ (Ephesians 5:20).

Thought: A true disciple is more than just a casual follower, for he must die to self, daily. It's not what's in your pocket that makes you thankful, but what's in your heart.

We should love in such a way that others can see that Christ truly lives today.

December

Scripture: In all thy ways acknowledge him, and he shall direct thy path (Proverbs 3:6).

Alas for the day! For the day of the LORD is at hand, and as; a destruction from the Almighty shall it come (Joel 1:15).

Thought: As we grow spiritually, we lose confidence in self, in our abilities, and develop a confidence in the Lord's wisdom in sustaining and guiding us.

I will, like Paul, forget those things that are behind and press forward.

You can reach your goal in life despite poverty as long as you keep your eyes upon it.

The judgment of God is upon all who oppose Him. Just believe Him and He will open up our understanding; just ask Him and He will give us wisdom and knowledge.

We Believe: The Bible is the inspired, infallible Word of God, written by holy men of old as they were moved by the Holy Ghost. "Knowing this first that, no prophecy of the scripture is of any private interpretation. For the prophecy came not in old time by the will of man: but holy men of God spoke as they were moved by the Holy Ghost" (II Peter 1:20–21).

<u>*The 21st Century Millennium Church Must Be&*</u>

Bishop William A. Ellis, DD Pastor
Apostolic Pentecostal Church of Morgan Park: Inc.

As I conclude this tribute, I would like to introduce the man our emeritus pastor 20 plus years ago introduced as his successor to reign in his stead as shepherd of God's people. Bishop E., as he likes to be called (because he has been set free), is moving us from tradition to revelation. Bishop William A. Ellis is the man of God chosen to lead God's people like Joshua after Moses. I hold a personal gratitude for Bishop Ellis because whenever he speaks of Suffragan Bishop Robert A. Baggett Sr., he says our retired pastor. Bishop Ellis is a man who believes in giving honor where honor is due.

Bishop Ellis has brought us into the 21st century through preaching on the 21st century millennium church and the power it must have in order to impact the world and lead souls out of darkness. Bishop Ellis is noted for joyfully entering to the spirit of worship and praise. He exhorts that we were born to worship the King regardless of our cares and the trials of life. He teaches that God will remove anything that keeps you from worshipping Him. Leave it behind he says; be honest with yourself. Pressure can drive you closer to God or away from God. Tell God, here I am, use me. Your destiny is in your hand.

Bishop Ellis challenges us to remember that this is a faith walk. He believes that the spirit of God will convict us when we fail God, as well as lead us to repentance. He urges us to pray that God will pull down the strongholds in our lives because strongholds are where Satan hides. He challenges us to say to ourselves, I have too much God in me to go down. The Holy Ghost is not just for a few, but for all. Bishop Ellis constantly reminds us that the church cannot lose focus during these turbulent times.

In accordance with his apostolic heritage naturally and spiritually, Bishop Ellis proclaims that we have access to Jesus through the baptism of water, in the name of Jesus. Some of his most powerful messages were: If You Wait on God, He'll Give You Double; Whatever God Says, Do It Because, you Can't See What's Down the Line; Some People Don't Understand That He Was Wounded for Us. Know That You're Chosen.

The Church Is the Only Hope for This World. Bishop Ellis further proclaims that: You Must Believe in God to survive; Believe in What You Ask, Exercise Your Faith in God, God Will Do the Impossible, Faith Sees a Way Out, Ask God to Kill the Flesh So You Can Survive.

Under a powerful and dynamic anointing Bishop Ellis is committed to crying loud and he spares not declaring that: We must Be Glad for The Saints; Somebody Prayed for You; The Lord Judges Your Heart, Not Your Action; Self- denial Is The First Step in Becoming Like Christ; The Life of Christ Gives You Humility; Keep The Fear of God in Your Heart; Don't Let Satan Have a Seat In Your House; Ask God to Keep Your Heart Clean; Your Miracle Is at the Door; It's Time to Answer the Door, and Excuse Me, I've Got to Get My Blessing!

First Lady Elaine Baggett, "Red": The promises of the Lord are of no avail to me except as I Apply, and appropriate them by faith. In my daily walk, I shall be victorious only to the degree that I trust in Him. He can help me only as I ask. He shall meet me at every point where I put action alone side my prayers. Only as I walk shall the waters of grief be parted before me.

Our Sister Elaine Baggett went home November 2014

Commemorate: **The Baggett**

AUTHOR BIOGRAPHY

Rose Love is a single mom, author of three other books and a retired nurse. She received her registered nurse certificate from Malcolm X College, her BSN and N.P. certification from Purdue University; a devoted Christian since 1973. She was eager to learn after not being in a church for thirteen years. The Baggett loved her as a daughter; and under their leadership she developed in the Lord. She had a ritualistic urgency to record and hoards everything. She was a choir member, head of the health professional, worked on the church bulletin, Sunday school secretary, and occasionally helped in the kitchen. The book is a twenty eight year commemorated excerpts of history. She is presently at Victory Apostolic Church in Matteson, IL.